SHADOW WOLF

ALSO BY ALICIA MONTGOMERY

THE TRUE MATES SERIES

Fated Mates

Blood Moon

Romancing the Alpha

Witch's Mate

Taming the Beast

Tempted by the Wolf

THE LONE WOLF DEFENDERS SERIES

Killian's Secret

Loving Quinn

All for Connor

THE TRUE MATES STANDALONE NOVELS

Holly Jolly Lycan Christmas

A Mate for Jackson: Bad Alpha Dads

TRUE MATES GENERATIONS

A Twist of Fate

Claiming the Alpha

Alpha Ascending

A Witch in Time

Highland Wolf

Daughter of the Dragon

Shadow Wolf

A Touch of Magic

Heart of the Wolf

THE BLACKSTONE MOUNTAIN SERIES

The Blackstone Dragon Heir

The Blackstone Bad Dragon

The Blackstone Bear

The Blackstone Wolf

The Blackstone Lion

The Blackstone She-Wolf

The Blackstone She-Bear

The Blackstone She-Dragon

This is a work of fiction. Names, characters, businesses, places, events, locales, and incidents are either the products of the author's imagination or used in a fictitious manner. Any resemblance to actual persons, living or dead, or actual events is purely coincidental.

SHADOW WOLF

TRUE MATES GENERATIONS BOOK 7

ALICIA MONTGOMERY

CHAPTER ONE

THE LONGER HE STAYED HERE, THE MORE MARC Delacroix realized that Lycans were not meant for the dry desert heat, and certainly not those who grew up in the wet, humid bayous of Louisiana. His inner wolf grumbled unhappily as a hot breeze hit them in the face.

Yes, it's uncomfortable, but would you rather be back there?

The wolf lay down and let out a defeated whine.

Yes, the deserts of Zhobghadi were too dry, the sun too bright, and the temperatures unbearable. But he would rather be here than stuck back in the hellhole he had called a home.

"If you think any louder, you'll wake Caspar up."

Delacroix blinked. "Apologies, Your Majesty."

Queen Desiree of Zhobghadi, formerly Desiree Desmond Creed of the New York Lycan clan, smirked up at him as she lay her infant son in his stroller, pulling the hood down to protect him from the blazing sun. "No jokes today, Delacroix? Are you sure you're not sick?"

The gentle teasing in her voice made the corners of his

mouth turn up involuntarily. "I'm feeling just fine, *mon petite*."

Normally, he wouldn't dare call the queen and mate to a dragon king such a nickname, but they were alone as they went for their mid-morning stroll in the royal gardens. *Non*, he liked his hide unburnt. But after a year of guarding the new young royal, they had certainly become close, along with another Lycan from her former clan, Jacob Martin.

When Desiree Creed became queen of the tiny independent nation of Zhobghadi, her father, Sebastian Creed, had asked that Delacroix and Jacob accompany his daughter in order to watch over her and ease her transition into her new life. It was not only a great honor, but now, he had another powerful man ingratiated to him. While Delacroix was, technically, bound to the New York clan, he was allowed to go to Zhobghadi, with the caveat that he could be recalled anytime. That bargain he had struck with Nick Vrost was rock solid.

"Then you're worried about going back to New York."

And now the piper had come for payment. Two days ago, Vrost had sent the message that he was to return to America ASAP to join the Guardian Initiative, the special task force formed by the Alpha to fight their enemies.

"Me, worried?" He snorted to make his point. "I'll miss this position. It's practically a vacation." Glancing over at the covered stroller, his thoughts turned to the young prince and heir, not even three months old. "Watching over His Highness is one of the cushiest jobs I've had." Though the thoughts of his previous jobs tried to surface in his mind, he pushed them away. His wolf growled, but he managed to calm it down. "Now I'll have to do real work," he said with a forlorn sigh.

"And my female staff will miss your charming ways," she replied in a wry tone. "Though I'll be glad for the peace when you do leave. You know, you have every eligible woman in the palace sighing after you."

"And I enjoy having them sigh after me."

"Yet the only thing I hear are complaints about no one has yet to snag you."

He wagged his eyebrows at her. "Ah, but with so many women, there is no need to choose just one, *non?*"

She raised a brow at him. "Did you choose any at all?"

"I don't kiss and tell, *mon petite.*"

"So, you haven't chosen at all."

The comment came from nowhere and hit its mark, catching him so off guard that he couldn't stop from wincing. Yes, he certainly wasn't lacking in attention from women, and he could have his pick of the beautiful women in the palace. *Could* being the operative word. "Any other employer would have complained that I would have been unprofessional if I went after every available female around."

"I'm not just your employer, Delacroix." Her expression turned serious. "I'd like to think I was your friend too."

Though they—him, the queen, and Jacob—had never mentioned it out loud, there had been a friendship between them since the beginning that didn't have to be said. "I'm lucky you count me as a friend, Majesty."

She sighed. "And up goes that wall again."

"Wall?"

Hand on her cocked hip, she stared at him. "You have this

easygoing charm that most people fall for. Most think you shallow and that there's nothing underneath that smile, especially with the way you flirt with anything in a skirt. But you can't fool me. I've known you too long, Delacroix. And I know what I saw and what I felt when you took me into the shadows."

"I am shallow." It was almost automatic, the way his defenses came up. The smile on his face widened so much that he thought his face would crack. "There's nothing more to say."

"I've been around your kind my whole life. Why won't you admit it?"

"Admit what?"

"What you are," she stated. "You're a hybrid. Half Lycan, half warlock. That's why you can do magic."

He huffed, but did not answer her. Usually, he parried inquiries about his nature, but then again, no one had ever asked him directly.

"I know the council views your kind warily," she continued. "But it's not like anyone's going to treat you differently. My best friends are hybrids and use their powers to protect our kind. Is it so bad to admit it?"

He bit the inside of his cheek to keep from saying anything. Yes, powers could be wielded for good, but they could also be abused.

"C'mon, D. It's nothing to be ashamed of."

"I'm not ashamed," he stated.

"Then what's wrong? Why won't you just say you're a hybrid and be done with it? It's obvious that's why Vrost recruited you."

Recruit. *Right*. "It's not what you think."

"Were your parents ... did something happen to your

witch or warlock parent, which is why you didn't realize you were a hybrid?"

"I don't know."

"You don't know?" Her expression was genuinely puzzled. "What do you mean?"

"I never knew them." He swallowed hard, feeling his wolf go still at the mention of his parents. "I was orphaned and taken in by the Pont Saint-Louis clan. If I am what you say I am, then there would be no one to confirm." In fact, he'd never met a hybrid until he'd been paired with Jacob, who had the ability to create and manipulate fire.

A gentle hand landed on his shoulder. "I'm so sorry. I didn't realize—Oh God, I'm so insensitive! I thought you were just being mysterious."

He hesitated, but he trusted her. And he would be gone here in a few days, so there would be no harm in revealing more. "I was about nine or ten when the shadows ... called to me." It was difficult to describe the feeling. It was like a pull, small at first, but growing bigger each day. The dark corners, whispering his name until he couldn't ignore it. "I ... disappeared into the shadow of this big oak tree on clan property. Then I reappeared a few feet away, from the shadows of an old shed."

"You must have been scared."

Actually, he wasn't. It had felt *right*. However, it was what happened after that was all wrong. When it had been discovered what he could do ... well, Remy Boudreaux was a bastard, and the fact that Delacroix was a child didn't matter to him. No, he only cared about getting what he wanted, even if it meant making others do his dirty work.

Delicate brows drew together, and her light green eyes

pleaded at him. "I'm sorry for bringing it up. I understand why you might not want to talk about it. But your abilities ... they could turn this war around for us."

This damn war with the mages, he growled inwardly. Granted, it was the mages who sought the destruction of his kind, and the Lycans were just trying to defend themselves. Still, he thought leaving his old clan behind would end the fighting and bloodshed. When he had made that pact with Nick Vrost, he didn't realize he would be exchanging one master for another. The violence was exhausting, and he'd already paid so many times, as if his very nature was a crime. When would it be enough?

"But he doesn't want to go."

The sound of the low, masculine voice never failed to make his wolf uneasy, and if he were honest, himself. Turning toward the source of the words, he straightened his spine and bowed his head. "Your Majesty."

King Karim stood in the entryway to the garden, dressed in his formal military tunic decorated with medals on the chest. His mere presence agitated him and his wolf, even after all this time, which was probably because the king was one of only two dragon shifters in the world. The power he held—both as ruling monarch of Zhobghadi and the animal he kept tightly reined in himself—would have cowered anyone, yet the moment his gaze landed on his queen, he was a completely changed man. The seriousness on his face disappeared, leaving only tenderness and warmth.

"*Habibti*," he murmured against her temple as he walked to her and bent down. "How is your day?"

"I'm great." She leaned against him, and his posture

relaxed. "Caspar is napping," she nodded at the stroller next to her.

"Don't wake him up; he'll only get cranky later." He turned to Delacroix, his face turning serious again. "I could ask Vrost if he could spare you for another year, at least until Caspar's first birthday. I'm sure Creed could speak on your behalf as well."

"That's kind of you, Your Majesty." He tipped his chin down reverently. "But it would only delay the inevitable."

"I hate that now I must lose *two* of my trusted guards," the king grumbled.

As soon as Delacroix received his marching orders from Vrost, Jacob had elected to go back to New York, not just to go back to his job at Lone Wolf Investigations, but to join the Guardian Initiative as well. He reasoned that it was time for him to go back home and that he was bored with life at the palace and wanted to be in the thick of the action. Delacroix wished he was as eager to fight, but he was glad his one true friend was going back with him.

"I am curious though." King Karim's blue eyes pierced into him. "What made you decide to pledge to New York?"

"He's not pledged yet," Queen Desiree explained. "He's a transfer, and unless he's a legacy transfer—meaning he had a parent or grandparent originally in the clan—it takes a few years. Five or six, I think."

"Five. I was a few weeks in before I came here. It was made clear to me by Vrost that my time here would not be counted." But, as soon as he reached New York soil, he would certainly be counting down to the last second until it was over. The reason he didn't mind going back was that the sooner he could start his service to the New York clan, the sooner he could finish it.

"So, why the move?" the king repeated. "What did Vrost offer you that your original clan could not?"

Delacroix pursed his lips, wondering what was the most diplomatic way he could tell the monarch to mind his own business.

"Darling." Queen Desiree placed a hand on his chest. "I think we've asked enough questions. How about we head back to our apartments, and we can have coffee until Caspar wakes up after his nap?" Keen light green eyes turned to Delacroix. "Can you meet me at the eastern doors at half past two? I'll need you to accompany me to my meeting at the university."

The tightness in his chest eased, and he was grateful to the queen for not making him reveal any more about his past. He had already revealed more to her than he had to anyone, and it was vital no one knew about his life before now. About the things he'd done. "As you wish, Your Majesty."

"Are you coming back with us?" King Karim asked with a cock of his head.

"I shall follow, Your Majesty. I would like to enjoy the desert air for a few more moments."

The king's brows knitted together, but he said nothing as he led his wife and child back into the palace.

Delacroix turned around, turning his face up to the bright burning sun. Yes, he would miss this place. In the short time he'd been here, he'd become comfortable living in Zhobghadi. It was far removed from anything he'd known, and if anyone had told him that his life would be this way a few years ago, he wouldn't have believed them.

But this place wasn't home. He couldn't even dare dream of it as such, or any place, really. The bayou wasn't home, and New York would never be home. New York was a way out. Many Lycans would have given their right arm to have been given an opportunity to be part of a powerful clan, but as soon as he was freed from his obligation, he would leave and become a Lone Wolf.

Not many Lycans could keep up with such a lifestyle—not having a permanent place to live or a clan to support them, constantly trying to pass as human. But the Lone Wolf life had something no clan could give him—freedom. The freedom to do what he pleased, when he pleased. Because he'd rather die than be under the thumb of any Alpha. Never again. And his wolf agreed wholeheartedly.

———

It didn't take too long for Delacroix and Jacob to settle their affairs in Zhobghadi. While they had been integrated into life at the palace, there was no one either would consider a close friend. They were well-acquainted with the Almoravid, the elite superhuman guards who protected the royal family having been training with them, but the language barrier made it difficult to make friends.

There were two people that had been difficult to say goodbye to. The first was Princess Amaya, King Karim's young sister. The princess had been distraught as he and Jacob watched over her as closely as they did the queen. She had come to think of them as "her" bodyguards and friends too. She had cried when she heard the news and even begged them to stay, but eventually, she had accepted it, though only because Queen Desiree promised to bring her to New York for a visit soon.

The second person was Ramin, King Karim's ward, whom the two Lycans had taken under their wing. The young man was strong and ambitious and was determined to join the ranks of the Almoravid someday. He and Jacob had trained the eager young man, and Delacroix could already tell that he would achieve his goal and maybe even become captain of the guard. Ramin took the news of their impending departure well, thanking them both for the additional training and sparring that would surely help him within the coming months as he prepared for his exams.

There was a small, private feast in their honor the night before they left. The captain of the Almoravid had been there, as well as most of the palace staff that they worked with. There was much feasting and drinking, and during the after party, he had rebuffed the advances of a particular amorous and drunk handmaiden who tried to put her hands down his pants. Jacob had merely shaken his head and laughed at him.

It wasn't that he didn't like women or sex. Once upon a time, he was up to his ears in willing women. And although he still enjoyed the flirting and attention, since he left Pont Saint-Louis, he kept his focus razor sharp on his eventual goal of freedom. Sure, he'd let Nick Vrost and the other Lycans think he was some kind of flirt, but the truth was, he hadn't been with a woman for more than a year. Being considered a shallow man whore was just one more way he could blend into the background—stay out of sight, unimportant, and serve his time until he could gain what he wanted most. Sex and women were too messy, and there was a danger to forming an attachment that could distract him.

"You okay, man?" Jacob asked.

Jolted out of his thoughts, he turned to his companion. *"Oui, mon ami."*

"We're about to land." The young man clicked his seatbelt on. "I can't believe we'll be landing in New York in a couple of minutes. Man, I'm going to miss living like this." His hands gripped the soft, buttery leather of his seat.

Sebastian Creed himself had sent his private plane to pick them up, saving them the trouble of several connecting flights seeing as Zhobghadi had no international airport. No expense had been spared on the interior of the plane, nor with the service and food. This was only the second time he'd flown private and probably the last. "Should have had one more glass of champagne," he joked.

Landing was smooth, and immigration formalities at the private airstrip in New Jersey where they landed had been conducted on-board as the plane sat on the tarmac. Gathering up his duffel bag, he followed Jacob out of the plane. As he descended down the steps, his gaze immediately went to the man standing next to the dark SUV, his arms crossed over his chest, obviously waiting for them. He was a couple inches taller than Delacroix and wore an expensive, well-fitting dark suit. Delacroix tried not to show any emotion as their eyes met, but it was hard not to bristle when confronted with those ice blue eyes that seem to bore into him.

"Welcome back." Nick Vrost unfolded his arms. "Glad to see you *both* made it."

His frosty gaze lingered on Delacroix, which made him

snort loudly. As if he would back out on his word. A bargain was a bargain.

"Thanks for coming to greet us, *Al Doilea*," Jacob said, using the honorific Lycans used for their Beta.

"Of course, though you might be disappointed to know I'm taking you straight to HQ. Your mother, in particular, was not happy you wouldn't be coming home right away."

Jacob winced. "I'll be sure to visit her, er, soon."

Delacroix suppressed a laugh. Mrs. Martin had seemed like a nice woman and all, at least from the short video chats where he'd said hello to her, but Jacob felt smothered by his mother's attentions. "I'm the baby of the family," he had explained some time ago. "And she can't seem to accept that I'm a grown man. Parents, you know?"

Actually, he didn't, but he didn't say anything since Jacob hadn't known anything about his past at the time. Did he want a mother who would smother him with love and attention? At this point in his life, he wasn't sure.

Vrost motioned for them to get into the SUV and soon they were driving toward the city. "Are we headed to Fenrir Corp.?" Jacob asked. The Fenrir Corporation building on Madison was not only the headquarters for the massive international conglomerate, but also unofficially, for the New York clan. Fenrir's CEO, Lucas Anderson, was also their Alpha.

"Not quite." Vrost didn't elaborate, and his gaze covered by the sunglasses he put on. As they approached the city, he couldn't help but feel wonder as the skyline appeared ahead. While New York was only his temporary home, there was just something about it that was both intimidating and comforting, especially after a year of seeing nothing but sand for miles on end.

As the SUV emerged from the Lincoln tunnel, the vehicle went south, away from the Fenrir Corp. building and The Enclave, the mini-city on the Upper West Side that served as the home for most of the New York clan. He and Jacob looked at each other, but it was obvious Vrost would offer no other explanation.

They were soon in the trendy district of Tribeca, and the car turned east, the Brooklyn Bridge clearly ahead of them as they made their way through a maze of smaller side streets.

Delacroix frowned as they pulled into an alleyway with a dead end. "Where are we—*mon Dieu!*"

Jacob, who had been sitting in the back, unbuckled his seatbelt and grabbed the front seat. "Mr. Vrost, what the—"

Vrost remained cool and calm as he stepped on the gas and the SUV sped up—straight toward the wall.

"You're crazy!" Delacroix closed his eyes and braced himself, waiting for the impact—but there was none. "What the fuck?"

The vehicle screeched to a halt, and when he opened his eyes and saw they were very much unharmed and not flat as pancakes against a brick wall, let out a soft curse. "You didn't think to warn us first?"

Cool as a cucumber, Vrost took off his sunglasses, his ice blue eyes filled with what seemed like amusement. "And miss all the fun?" He unbuckled his seatbelt. "Welcome to the secret headquarters of the Guardian Initiative, gentlemen. Secret being the operative word, hence why I couldn't tell you where we were headed. The wall we went through was one of the many magical enchantments we put in place to hide this place from humans and the mages."

As they exited the vehicle, Delacroix looked around. They seemed to be in some kind of indoor garage, the only source of light coming from hanging overhead industrial lights. Vehicles were parked next to the SUV, including several motorcycles, two vans, an armored military vehicle, and even a Winnebago.

"Where the heck are we?" Jacob asked. "I mean, what part of Manhattan are we? Are we even still in New York?"

Vrost cocked his head. "Follow me." He led them toward an elevator in the corner and pressed his palm against the sensor by the door. After a soft whirr and a high-pitched beep, the doors opened. He pointed forward. "After you."

They stood in the elevator as Vrost pressed the second to last button on the panel. The elevator ascended, and a few seconds later, the doors opened, and they stepped out. The space looked like a normal office, with desks and computers and people typing away at keyboards in their cubicles. But from the energy in the air, it was obvious there was more to this place than what it seemed.

"Whoa!" Jacob hurried over to one of the large windows. "We're in the middle of the water. That's New York. And Brooklyn's over there." He looked at Vrost, his eyes wide. "Are we—"

"In one of the stone towers of the Brooklyn Bridge, yes."

Delacroix followed Jacob, and peered out of the pane. However, there was something strange about this window. He poked a finger at the window. "This isn't glass."

Vrost shook his head. "No, it's not. When we decided this would be our headquarters, one of the problems we encountered was that the entire structure was solid, which was great for defense, but that meant we couldn't see what was going on outside. Plus, it made the place pretty gloomy. So, we installed 4K screens that have a direct feed to the outside to mimic windows."

"Cool." Jacob tipped his chin. "So, this place is our war room."

"You could say that. This floor is central operations. Above us is the actual war room and command, while we have the training rooms and dorms in the two floors below us."

"How did you fit all that in the tower?" Jacob asked.

"Magic," Vrost explained. "Daric was able to find a magic spell that could expand the space on the inside. I don't know how it works, and it cost us a pretty penny, but it was worth it. This place is more secure than Fort Knox. Now, I need to introduce you to some people, though you already know most of them, Jacob."

He led them to one of the enclosed offices and opened the door. It was a small, cramped space, filled with PC towers of varying sizes along two sides of the room and a wall of monitors in the middle. There was a single desk in the middle that had a laptop, and a large, beat-up leather chair turned away from them.

"You've reached Acme Proctologists, where we promise you a *thoroughly* good time. How may I direct your call?"

Vrost's gaze slid heavenwards in an exasperating manner and cleared his throat. "Lizzie," he said in a warning voice.

"....no really, sir ... that's right. Would you like to make an appointment?" The chair swiveled around, revealing its occupant—a cute redhead with sparkling blue eyes full of mischief as she spoke into a cell phone. "You don't have to be shy, sir. All our doctors are gentle."

"Lizzie," Vrost repeated.

The woman—more like a girl, really—bit her lip as she tried to smother a giggle. "No need to take that tone with me, sir. I already deal with assholes all day."

"*Martin.*" Vrost warned.

Martin? Delacroix turned to Jacob, who only gave him the same exasperated look on Vrost's face.

With a delighted cackle, the redhead put the phone down. "Wha—Oh! *Al Doilea!*" She shot up from her seat, then froze when her gaze landed on Jacob. "And—*Oh, my God!* Runt, you're home!" Her face turned from embarrassment to shock to excitement as she launched herself at Jacob, leaping up at him to wrap her arms around his neck.

"Runt?" Delacroix asked as Jacob tried to untangle the young woman from his body.

"I—get-off-me-you-crazy-woman! Argh! Stop!"

"*Aww*, can't I express how much I've missed my baby brother?" She let go of him, then punched him in the arm. "Nice to see you, runt."

Jacob scowled and rubbed his arm. "Don't call me that. I'm more than a foot taller than you and outweigh you by a hundred pounds."

"But you'll always be the baby of the family." Her face scrunched up as she pinched his cheeks.

Vrost cleared his throat. "I'll leave you all to get acquainted while I round up Wyatt and Mika."

"Oh, of course, Mr. Vrost."

The Beta gave Delacroix a warning look before turning

on his heel and leaving the office. The redhead turned to Delacroix. "I'm Lizzie Martin, head of tech around here, and Jacob's sister."

"So I gathered." Jacob had mentioned he had two siblings, but didn't give any more details. He shook the female's hand. "Marc Delacroix."

"I thought that's who you might be." Arctic blue eyes peered up at him. "I've heard a lot about you."

Dressed in a short plaid skirt, a T-shirt with a cartoon alpaca on the front, and knee-high boots, she looked out of place here, but he'd learned long ago not to judge people by their looks. He turned on his megawatt smile automatically, and his eyes darted up and down her curvaceous body. "Funny. Jacob's never mentioned his sister was so ... interestin'."

"Keep those eyes at an appropriate level, Delacroix," Jacob warned. "Unless you want me to pull them out of their sockets."

Lizzie rolled her eyes and then pulled something out of her pocket—a lollipop, which she proceeded to unwrap and suck into her mouth. "Please, Jacob. I can take care of myself. You know, the last time a guy tried anything funny, he ended up on the FBI's Most Wanted list."

He took a step closer. "Ah, you are giving me a challenge then?" Her scent was pleasant enough—a sweetness that smelled generic but his Lycan senses detected the wolf in her and a hint of something different, similar to the way Jacob smelled. Probably the same thing that marked him as a hybrid, but it wasn't enough to rouse his wolf, who, during all this time, remained passive and indifferent to their new surroundings.

"Oh, you charmer, you!" Mirth made her arctic blue eyes light up. "You don't want to mess with me. I can make you hurt in different ways."

Which of course only piqued his curiosity. "Oh, really?" He reached out to touch a lock of red hair intending to brush it off her shoulder. "I—"

The low growl that followed made his hackles raise and pull his hand back immediately. Turning to the door, Vrost stood there with another man, who stalked into the room like a predator who'd found his next victim. He was at least half a foot taller than Delacroix, and just as wide, though it was hard to tell with the way he seemed to puff out his chest and shoulders. Green eyes so light they were almost yellow blazed with an icy fury that was directed straight at him. Familiar eyes.

"*Ahem.*" Vrost stepped between them. "Delacroix, you've met Wyatt before, haven't you? He's our operations manager."

Wyatt Creed. Queen Desiree's brother. Ah, that's why he was familiar; he was practically a younger carbon copy of his father. He'd seen the man twice in Zhobghadi—once during the wedding and another time after Prince Caspar was born —though he had never spoken with him. The middle Creed offspring had a superior air about him that seemed to say he was too good to speak to anyone beneath him, like bodyguards and servants. Which had been a puzzle to say the least, because the rest of the Creed family had been warm and friendly to everyone. He'd found Wyatt to be cold and stuck up, but never confrontational. What could have provoked him?

Lizzie pulled the lollipop from her mouth. "Can we get on with it, please? I have work to do."

As the female turned on her heel and walked back behind her desk, Wyatt's eyes tracked her movements. *Huh.* Definitely a piece of information he was going to put away for now.

"Where's the boss?" Jacob plopped down on the nearest chair in front of Lizzie's desk, so Delacroix followed suit and sat beside him. Wyatt didn't make a move from where he stood by the door, but merely crossed his arms over his chest, his entire body going stiff.

"Mika's running late today," Vrost explained. "But she told me to go ahead and start without her, and she'll catch up. So, you two, welcome back to New York."

Nothing would have pleased Delacroix more than to wipe that smug smile off the Beta's face. "Glad to be back," he shot back.

Vrost seemingly ignored the sarcasm in his tone. "Now that you're back, we need to get you up to speed as soon as possible. We are at war with the mages, make no mistake. With the defeat of Stefan, the master mage thirty years ago, we assumed that they'd been eradicated. But as we know, they'd only been biding their time, growing their strength and forces, recruiting among witches around the world. In some cases, they've taken entire covens, by persuasion or force. Not only that, they've been searching for the three artifacts of Magus Aurelius, magical objects that have so much power that they could put the entire world under their control. They have one, the necklace that can control humans, and we have one, the dagger of Magus Aurelius, safely tucked away in a secret location, but they're doing everything in their power to steal ours.

"The Alpha has refused to stay passive, and we've hunted down every mage coven we could find, but it's like the more we take down, more spring up somewhere else. Between trying to find the last artifact, protecting ourselves and the dagger, and hunting down the mages, our forces are spread too thin. That's why we've recalled you two." His icy blue gaze, however, focused on Delacroix. "We need all hands on deck if we're going to end this war soon. Your abilities and your training with the Almoravid will be invaluable to us."

An acrid taste built up in his throat. Once again, he and his abilities would be used and abused, made to fight in a war that had nothing to do with him. In leaving the Pont Saint-Louis clan for New York, he was only exchanging one master for another. At least in Zhobghadi, he had been at peace.

"You look like you have something to say, Delacroix."

Vrost's tone was as chilly as his icy stare, daring him to object. But he couldn't. The bargain had been made, and the New York clan owned him for the next five years. However, he wouldn't act like some obedient puppy, begging for its master's approval.

"Don't make much difference to me one way or the other." He stretched out on the chair languidly, placing his hands behind his head and ankles crossed in front of him.

"Delacroix's job at the palace was mostly to sit and look pretty," Jacob joked. "And cause fights among the queen's handmaidens."

"I'm more of a lover than a fighter." He wiggled his eyebrows at Lizzie, who ignored him in favor of scrolling on her phone. He felt the hairs on the back of his neck prickle in awareness like someone was staring at him, and he didn't need to turn his head to know where those particular daggers were coming from.

"You'll follow orders, Delacroix," Vrost said in a warning voice. "If you know what's good for you."

Like he needed it rubbed in his face some more. "I'll follow your orders, but I don't have any skin in this game, so don't expect me to give more than I have to or give a rat's ass about this war of yours."

"Actually, it's everyone's war. The goddamn mages are out to destroy every last Lycan on earth."

The voice was low and husky, and his entire body froze as if a giant hand had seized him in an iron grip. When his head swung toward the newcomer entering the room, the first thing he noticed were her eyes. Green, like the color of emeralds but the hardness of diamonds. Long, jet black hair was pulled back in a braid that swung over one shoulder. She was of medium height and slim build, though her white button-down shirt and black trousers didn't hide the feminine curves underneath.

And then, something strange happened. Something that, as far as he could remember, had never happened before. His inner wolf perked up, and its attention fixed on *her*.

Who was this woman?

CHAPTER TWO

MIKA WESTBROOKE HADN'T EVEN OPENED HER EYES that morning when that dark heavy feeling came over her.

Today wasn't going to be a good day. Most days were okay, some were good, some were bad, but she knew *this* particular day would be terrible.

She had stayed up the night before, willing herself not to sleep as if doing so would stop the inevitable. That somehow, if she never fell asleep, this day wouldn't come. Exhaustion had come over her, and sleep eventually took over, which meant she had missed her alarm.

Any other day and she would have cursed and jumped out of bed, scrambling to get ready. But then again, any other day she would have never missed her alarm. As head of the Guardian Initiative, she didn't have the luxury to dillydally, not when their missions were so critical.

Not today. Today of all days, she took her time. Sending Nick Vrost a message that she would be running late, she took her time getting ready, as the dark fog that seemed to surround her today made her move sluggishly, not caring about the time.

Eventually, she got herself out of her apartment in The Enclave, drove herself to the Brooklyn Bridge HQ, and finally made it into the office only an hour late. She told Nick to start without her, so she wasn't surprised that they were already in the middle of the meeting when she walked into Lizzie's office. Not wanting to disturb them, she quietly crept inside, but unfortunately, the first words she heard cracked the already precarious hold she had on her emotions.

"I'm more of a lover than a fighter."

"You'll follow orders, Delacroix,"

"I'll follow your orders, but I don't have any skin in this game, so don't expect me to give more than I have to or give a rat's ass about this war of yours."

Anger reverberated in her chest. Who *the fuck* did this man think he was? Before she knew it, the caustic words flew out of mouth. "Actually, everyone's got skin in this game. The goddamn mages are out to destroy every last Lycan on earth."

And then something happened that caught her off guard.

Dark eyes slammed into her, making her ... feel things she never thought she'd feel again. Never wanted to feel again, at least not with anyone new. Heat uncurled from her stomach, and first, she thought it was anger, but no. It was that uncomfortable feeling of *need*.

Get a grip, Westbrooke. He's just another cocky male you'll have to deal with.

This was normal, she told herself. Because the asshole in question making her feel this way was unusually good looking. Pitch-black hair that matched his eyes. Tight white T-shirt stretched over the broadest shoulders she'd ever seen.

Tattoos covered what was exposed of his enormous arms. And, despite the dark beard that covered half his face, the grin making his sensuous mouth spread only made him more devilishly handsome. The man stood up and offered his hand.

Seemingly unperturbed by her reprimand, his smile grew wider. "Marc Delacroix, nice to make your acquaintance. And you are ...?"

Ah, so this was Delacroix, Nick's recruit. "Your *boss*," she shot back, arms stiffly at her sides. "And your worst nightmare if I ever catch you slacking off."

Now *that* wiped the infuriating smile off his face. "I think we got off on the wrong foot, *cher*. You don't know anythin' about me."

Her eyes narrowed at him. "I know enough about you, Delacroix." Nick had briefed her, of course. She knew the entire story of how the Cajun had come to New York and how desperate he had been to leave his former clan. Quite simply, they had him by his balls. "I don't care what you do on your off time, but when you're here, you're going to keep your head straight. A single mistake could cost the life of one my guys, and if that happens, I'm sending you back to whatever swamp you crawled out of."

She could feel everyone in the room practically flinch at her words, and much later, she would see how harsh she was. But not now. She couldn't take this maelstrom of emotions, not today of all days.

Delacroix's Adam's apple bobbed up and down as he swallowed. "Understood, ma'am."

Her she-wolf scratched at her furiously. *What the hell is wrong with you?* "Welcome back, Jacob." She pushed her wolf away, ignoring its protests. "I'm happy you decided to join us."

He grinned. "Can't let you guys have all the fun, now, can I?"

Mika was glad the youngest of the Martin siblings decided to join the Guardian Initiative, as they needed every advantage they could get. He'd been on her shortlist of candidates because of his powers but was disappointed to learn he'd been assigned to guard the newly crowned Queen Desiree. "Great. Now that I have everyone here, maybe we can get you up to speed and continue with our morning briefing."

Meetings at the Guardian Initiative were informal affairs, as they didn't really have the time or space to conduct elaborate gatherings. They usually met in her office upstairs, but she wanted to get this over with. "Let's start with the bad news ..."

Compartmentalization had never been a problem for her, something she'd been thankful for, especially in the last two years. That and the fact that she needed to do something—in this case, fight the mages—to keep her mind and hands busy or she would have sunk into a deep depression.

Today, however, she found herself distracted and annoyed. When Nick began to update them with news from the Alpha's office, she couldn't concentrate, as she felt like she was being watched. Turning her head, her gaze clashed with dark eyes. Heat crept up her neck, but she ignored him. But it didn't do any good as she felt him staring at her, even if she didn't look his way.

"....for now, we'll keep an eye on the situation." Nick turned to her. "Anything else, Mika?"

"There's the Russian situation." Ugh, *that* particular subject was going to ruin her day further. "But that's something you, the Alpha, and I need to talk about."

"I'll talk to him, and we can convene on the matter."

"Great. Wyatt," she began. "Get our new guys settled in. Jacob, I know you can stay with your parents, but we have living quarters here for anyone who wants to stay. It's not a five-star hotel, but it's clean and comfortable, similar to the ones at Fenrir."

"I'll take 'em," he said eagerly.

"You just don't want to live with Mom and Dad," Lizzie snickered which earned her a dirty look.

"You'll be staying there too," Nick said to Delacroix.

"Lucky me," the Cajun muttered. "And you, *cher*? Do we get to be neighbors? Perhaps I can borrow a cup of sugar sometime, *oui*?"

Desire shot straight to her core at the inviting tone of his voice. *The nerve of this bastard!* Ignoring him, she pivoted on her heel and walked out of Lizzie's office. As soon as she was far away enough, she took a deep breath of the artificial air-conditioned air, trying to calm herself. Her inner wolf, on the other hand, paced back and forth, almost chastising her.

How could someone she'd only met barely an hour ago tie her up in knots and make her wolf behave strangely? She'd always felt at peace with her inner animal, but this was the first time it seemed defiant, like a teenager testing its boundaries. However, it was like *she* was the teen. All hormones and no sense.

It's the lack of sex, she told herself. More than two years of celibacy was catching up with her. She was horny, and he was the first male she'd met that she wasn't related to or had worked with in her capacity as head of GI. Not yet anyway. But that would change soon.

She must have been standing there too long because a group of people standing by the watercooler in the corner was staring at her. Narrowing her eyes, she shot them glares of reproach, making them scurry back to their cubicles. With a silent satisfied harrumph, she strode toward the elevators and jabbed the call button. As she waited, that feeling came over her again—that someone was watching her.

A frisson of excitement shot up her spine, but she ignored it. Her enhanced hearing could pick up his heavy footsteps coming toward her. "Come on you damned thing," she muttered under her breath at the doors.

"*Cher*, I think we—"

Maybe God was looking down at her today because the silver doors slid open, and she hurried inside and pressed the button for the top floor. As she turned around, the sight of Delacroix's surprised face was the last thing she saw as the doors shut.

With a relieved sigh, she leaned against the wall, pressing her forehead to the cool metal. What was it about him that made her both uneasy and thrilled? Why was her inner wolf acting so strange? God, this was the worst timing for her to be feeling this way. *Please, not today.*

———

It was one of those workdays that seemed to last forever, but by the time she was finally leaving her office, Mika felt like it had ended too soon. That tightness that had been in her chest the entire day only gripped harder, but she knew she had to get through the rest of this day without breaking down. Clearing her head, she made her way to her car in the garage and drove out of HQ and into the streets of lower Manhattan. Swinging back, she actually had to cross over the Brooklyn Bridge to get to Flatbush.

After pulling into an empty street parking spot, she opened the trunk of her car and took out the six pack of craft beer she had placed there last night and walked toward the austere stone arches of the Holy Memorial Cemetery.

It was a beautiful, crisp fall afternoon, and the bright reds and golds of the foliage were on full display. Though her Lycan biology ensured her body was always at an even temperature, Mika clutched at the collar of her coat tight with one hand as a chill went through her. She took her time, taking in the peace and quiet of the cemetery as she made her way to the familiar row of headstones before finally stopping at the one near the end.

Joseph Allen Morgan
Beloved Son and Husband

"Hey, babe. Happy birthday."

She lay the six-pack—it had been Joe's favorite—by the headstone and knelt down, lovingly caressing the name carved into the gray granite. "I can't believe this is your third birthday up there." Which meant it had been more than two years since the car crash that killed him, the one that she survived because of her Lycan accelerated healing.

Clearing the lump in her throat, she continued. "I hope you're having a great time with all the angels. No, no," she shook her head, as if she could hear his deep voice protesting.

"I always believed you'd end up there. You're too good, you know. So selfless and caring. Everyone knew it, especially all those people you helped get back on their feet."

Joe had been director of a men's homeless shelter in Brooklyn and had been well-liked by everyone. He worked eighty hours a week caring for the residents, and sometimes even taking time during his weekends to help when they were shorthanded or if a resident was in trouble. The day of his funeral, over a hundred people had come to pay their respects.

"You were always too good, even for this world."

The month after he was buried, she'd come here every day, talking to him. Some people might have thought she was crazy, but coming here had helped her cope with the crushing sadness in those days. Her family and friends had been concerned, but they didn't interfere. As time went by, she knew she had to pick herself up and get on with her life. So she came less and less. It felt like a betrayal, but even she knew Joe wouldn't have wanted her to wallow in depression her whole life, no matter how tempting it was. But when would she truly feel like she was over it?

"I miss you, babe." She lay her head on the cold, hard stone. "Every day, I miss you."

Joe was the first serious relationship she'd ever had, serious enough that she had asked permission from the Lycan High Council to reveal her true nature to him after a year of living together. He'd been shocked when she had told him what she was, but it had never occurred to him to break up with her. He accepted her for what she was, even if there was a chance they might never have children.

No one knew why for sure, but Lycans had difficulty

conceiving. Most couples had one pup, if at all, and human–Lycan pairings always produced a fully human child. The one exception was True Mate pairing. True Mates, whether Lycan–Lycan or Lycan–human, always produced Lycan offspring during their first consummation.

Though they'd never said it, she'd always thought her parents had been disappointed she didn't wait for her True Mate. After all, Alynna and Alex Westbrooke had been the first True Mate couple of their generation, and before then, her mother was the product of True Mates as well. But what was there to wait for? Joe had been here, and he was perfect, and they were in love. Why would she wait for someone that might never come, when she had the one she wanted right in front of her?

Of course, she never thought she would lose him so soon. A drunk driver had plowed into their car on the highway as they were coming back from Long Island after a family get-together. While she had healed before the injuries became fatal, Joe died on impact. He had felt no pain, the doctors said. A small comfort at least.

If only they had waited another five minutes before leaving or left five minutes earlier. If only she had been the one driving. So many ifs and buts. It used to drive her crazy. But she accepted he was gone. The only *if* that wouldn't leave her mind was what if they at least had a baby, so she would have someone to love, a little piece of Joe left with her. The hardest part of losing him was the fact that in the three years they'd been married, they'd been trying for a baby with no success.

As if that wasn't bad enough, her relatives and friends had started pairing off, finding their own True Mates and having pups. All her cousins, even Isabelle, the youngest one of them, were popping out babies left and right. It wasn't that she was resentful of their luck, not at all. But it was like her biological clock began ticking desperately and wasn't giving up. If only—

Someone quietly clearing their throat behind her made her sit up quickly and turn her head. "Daric?"

The tall Viking-like man's sudden appearance didn't surprise her, after all, traveling long distances in the blink of an eye was one of the warlock's powers.

"I'm sorry to disturb you"—he glanced at Joe's headstone—"and today of all days. But we have to go *now*."

She shot to her feet. "What the hell is going on?"

"*He* had a vision." The warlock's words made her skin prickle. Before she could ask what the vision was, he reached out and grabbed her arm. "They're going to take the pups."

CHAPTER THREE

A COLD SENSATION WRAPPED AROUND MIKA AS THE cemetery shimmered away, and the ground underneath her disappeared. Three heartbeats later, her feet landed on solid ground, and a cacophony of noise assaulted her ears.

Her gaze cut through the chaos around them, her mind quickly assessing the situation. They were on the street just outside a pair of restaurants owned by the Alpha's extended family. By the entrance of Muccino's was New York's human Lupa, Sofia Anderson, her gun drawn as three men closed in on her, her other hand clutching a small, dark-haired infant close to her chest. Meanwhile, a few feet away was a humungous silver wolf with cobalt blue eyes growling, snapping at six armed figures dressed in black. Behind the wolf, loud cries came from the pup inside the car seat lying on its side on the ground.

"Fuck!" Adrenaline began to pump into her veins, ready to spring into action.

"More are coming," Daric said cryptically. "More than just you and I can handle."

"Get help." She was already hurtling forward. Darius—
the silver wolf—would be able to hold off his attackers, but
Sofia was human, and a single gunshot could end her and her
son, who had yet to develop accelerated healing. In the blink
of an eye, she took down the three men, the element of
surprise and Lycan speed on her side as she snapped each of
their necks with practiced efficiency.

Sofia's hand shook as she lowered her gun, her arm
clutching tighter around the infant slung to her chest. "Th-
thanks, Mika. Darius—"

She didn't even wait for the Lupa to finish as she leapt
toward the silver wolf, not that he needed her to fight his
battles. Darius Corvinus had been a cold-blooded killer
before he became consort to her cousin Adrianna
Anderson, New Jersey Alpha, but now that he was
protecting his pup, his viciousness would know no end. In
the short time since Mika arrived, three of the men had
already fallen, while he fought the rest simultaneously, his
Lycan speed making quick work of the rest. So instead,
Mika dove for the carrier, pulling it upright and
unstrapping the wailing child.

"There, there, Diana," she cooed as she pressed the pup
against her chest. The distinct scent of babies—talcum
powder, sweetness, and fresh linen—made her insides warm,
but also intensified the yearning to hold her own child.
"Aunty Mika's here. Shh." Diana Corvinus's cries quieted,
turning into soft hiccups.

The silver wolf stalked toward them nonchalantly as if he
hadn't left a pile of bloody bodies in his wake. Slowly, it
transformed back to human form, its limbs shortening, and
fur and snout receding. Darius's face was a mask of quiet

rage, and the waves of fury emanating from him made Mika's wolf back away cautiously.

"She's fine." She handed the child to Darius. "What happened?"

Sofia came up to them as she holstered her weapon. "We were all supposed to meet for dinner, but Lucas and Adrianna both got held up at Fenrir, so they said we should go ahead. We were just about to enter the restaurant when those guys showed up. They said to hand Alessandro and Diana over."

"How did you know to come?" Darius's accented voice was tense with a hint of a snarl.

"Daric came to get me. Our source had a vision that they were coming for the pups." For now, the identity of their "source" was only known to Lucas, Adrianna, and Mika. Gunnar Jonasson, Daric's youngest child, was a powerful hybrid who had visions of the future. Originally, Daric had hidden his son's abilities, fearful that they would be abused. However, when the Guardian Initiative was formed, he told the two Alphas and Mika because Gunnar had a vision about an attack on the Boston clan, which they were able to prevent. His predictions had been vital to their cause and had saved them many times, as well as aided them in ferreting out the location of the mages. "He also said—" The screeching of tires cut her off, and four black vans rounded the corner heading straight for them. "Shit! They're here."

"They?" Sofia said in an incredulous tone.

"Yeah. Reinforcements."

The vans stopped in the middle of the street, the doors sliding open even before the vehicles came to a halt.

Darius scanned the area. "I don't see any mages around."

Sofia pulled her gun out again. "Looks like the mages had their hired goons do this one."

"Good." From what they'd learned, their enemies had recruited blessed warlocks and witches—those who had active powers, like Daric—into their cause and turned them into mages which proved to be an advantage to them. Mika herself had encountered a mage who could control water and nearly drowned her.

"That means no teleporting either," Sofia observed. Another thing they'd learned—mages could somehow transport themselves over relatively short distances, but only if there were at least three of them to activate the spell. "But there's still too many of these guys."

"Daric went to get help."

As if on cue, the air around them shimmered, and the warlock himself appeared in front of them as well as about a dozen other Lycans from GI. "We're here."

"Take Sofia and the pups," Mika said, though Daric already had his hands stretched out. As he disappeared with the children, she glanced around. "Crap."

Four dozen men dressed in combat gear and armed with automatic rifles had surrounded them. But everyone who had arrived had seen their share of skirmishes, and they didn't need to wait for the signal to attack.

"Fire at will!" someone shouted.

Their enemies raised their weapons, but the Lycans were too fast. A few giant wolves leapt into action, taking as many as they could down as bullets whizzed by. Mika stayed in human form, preferring to fight hand-to-hand, plus, she had to be ready to issue commands if necessary which would have been difficult in her Lycan form.

"Motherfucker!" Pain shot down her left leg as a bullet ripped through her flesh. No matter, it would heal. Rage filled her as she stalked toward the man who still had his weapon pointed at her, and her inner wolf was reaching for the surface. His eyes went wide as she let out a loud growl, and he pulled the trigger again.

She braced for the impact of bullets, shutting her eyes tight as she leapt forward, ready to release her wolf. However, the only impact she felt was a strong, vice-like grip wrap around her stomach and pull back.

"What the—" She opened her mouth wide, trying to suck in the air that had been knocked out of her. When she was able to breathe, she realized everything had gone dark, like someone had turned off all the street lamps, the signs, even the moon and stars. There were silhouettes and forms around her, but it was as if a blanket covered her head. It was strange because as a Lycan, she could see pretty well in the dark. Her hearing, too, was muffled.

"Martinez!" she screamed as she recognized one of her agents. But he just ran past her as he lunged for one of the humans, like he didn't see or hear her.

What was going on?

Something pulled her back again until she was pressed against something hard. A wall? No, it was warm and—oh, dear Lord, that scent. Damp grass, smoke, and something she couldn't name, except it was like ... pure dark sex.

"Stay still, *cher*."

The damned Cajun. Though she wanted to struggle away from him, her body wouldn't obey. Hands gripped on her arms sent shocks of electricity through them.

"You are not used to the shadows." His voice was like warm honey, and her knees buckled.

"Th-the shadows?"

"Yes. It's my ... ability."

Ah yes, Nick told her about this. The power he possessed. "You have the power to go into the shadows?"

She felt the slightest brush of his cheek against hers. "Somethin' like that. But don't move too much. I don't want to lose you in here."

God, his presence, his voice, the warmth of his muscled body at her back made her want to melt into a puddle. Need clawed at her, and her inner wolf, which had been ready to fight and rip up their enemies just moments ago, suddenly found him very interesting. Its ears were perked up, full attention on him. "What the hell ...?"

The meaning of it all hit her so fast, it was as if the wind was knocked out of her for a second time.

Oh no.

No. No.

Despite all the chaos around them, her mind had pieced it all together. How could she ignore it when she'd heard it all her life? The stories of her parents, her grandparents, and the rest of the Lycans in their clan? The electric shock on first touch, the delicious scent that called to them, the way their wolves gravitated toward that one person like an irresistible force? There was only one person in the world who could elicit all that.

A True Mate.

"Are you all right?" he asked.

Was she all right? Goddamn him! "I'm ... what the hell is

happening? I mean, how come Martinez just blew past me like he didn't see me?"

"They can't see us here, in the shadows," he said. "You're safe."

Safe? *Right.* "I ... we need to help."

"You are injured." His voice was tight, as if he actually cared.

"And I'll heal, you know that." The bullet had gone through her leg, but she could feel the bleeding had stopped. "We need to help."

"They are fine. The humans are already pulling back."

Though her eyes strained to see clearly through the dark fog around them, Delacroix was right. Only a handful remained of the human forces, and even then, half of them had been sacrificed so the others could jump into their vans and make a getaway. Unfortunately, their side seemed to have suffered injuries, though no casualties.

"Mika ..." His lips were so near the shell of her ear, his breath hot on her skin. Lust crackled between them as if she could see the sparks. When did he plant his hand on her hip? Even through her clothes, the heat from his touch branded her as his fingers ran up the side of her stomach, leaving a trail of fire in its wake. Knuckles brushed below her breasts.

"Let me go," she whispered. "We should—"

The blanket of darkness over her disappeared as if it had been yanked back. She drew in the cool night air desperately into her lungs, and quickly broke away from Delacroix's grasp. Perhaps there was also something about being in the shadows with him that had amplified what she was feeling because out here, the pull to him felt dulled. It was still there, just less intense. Ignoring her wolf's yowling protests, she marched toward the tall figure standing in the middle of the street.

"You all right, Arch?" she asked, wincing as she saw the wound on his arm.

Arch Jones's unusual violet eyes twinkled as he flashed her a weak smile. "Yeah, it went through. And you?" He glanced down at her bloodied leg.

"Same. Dry cleaning bill's gonna be a bitch."

He glanced around at the carnage they had caused. "Same with the cleanup here."

She gave him a wry smile. "Well, that's why you're in charge of making sure the humans don't suspect a thing." Arch was not only their best agent, but also a smooth talker and born diplomat. He often liaised with authorities to help keep humans in the dark about their secret. That particular task had been increasingly difficult because of all the skirmishes with the mages, but he'd managed the task brilliantly so far.

"I've already given the police commissioner a call. The forgetting potions are ready to be administered to any humans who may have witnessed anything. Daric's transported the worst of the wounded to medical, and Cliff's getting everyone rounded up." He jerked a thumb behind him where Cliff Forrest, the head of their combat division, was kneeling down to check on one of their guys. "Are the pups safe?"

She nodded. "Thank God, yes." Adrenaline was slowly leaving her body, and exhaustion was creeping in.

He brushed a stray lock of hair from her forehead. "Are you sure you're okay."

"Yeah, I—"

A low growl from behind made her freeze. "Shouldn't you be headed to the doctor, *cher*?"

The hum of possessiveness in his tone sent a bolt of lust all the way to her core. Summoning up her annoyance, she turned to Delacroix. "I told you, I'm fine."

His scowl deepened when his gaze flickered to Arch, his lips curled into a half-snarl. "This senseless war ..."

"Senseless?" All feelings of lust dissolved, and she was reminded of his flippancy this morning. Good. It was best to remember what a good-for-nothing slacker he was with no moral compass. "They just tried to take two of our pups. Do you know what would have happened to them? To this clan if they succeeded?"

He reached out to her. "*Cher*, I—"

She slapped his hands away. "Stop. Just ... get away from me." She couldn't think, couldn't breathe when he was around. Her damn body—and wolf—focused on him, only him.

The shrill ring of her cellphone made her sigh in relief. Fishing it from her pocket, she didn't even bother to check who it was. "Westbrooke."

"Everyone all right?" came the tense voice of Lucas Anderson, Alpha of New York.

She winced, and Arch raised a brow at her. "Yes, Primul." Hearing her use the formal title for their Alpha made him step back. "No casualties on our side, but a few of them got away."

"I want those motherfuckers hunted down. No one gets away with trying to take my mate and son."

"We're doing our best, but we need to tend to our injured."

"Fine. But report to Fenrir as soon as you can. Adrianna and I will be here."

"Will do." After slipping her phone back into her pocket, she surveyed the scene before her—the destruction, the dead bodies, the Lycans who had transformed back into their human forms and were in various states of undress, not to mention the curious onlookers were starting to gather.

"Let's get to work," she told Arch. "And—" Oh. Delacroix was nowhere to be found. Huh. Figures. It was a good thing he's gone, she convinced herself. There was so much work to be done, and it was going to be a long night.

———

"Tell us everything that happened."

Lucas Anderson sat behind the large desk in his office, seemingly a vision of calmness. But there was no mistaking the power and fury he was trying to contain, his mismatched eyes—one blue, one green—blazed with a fire that could explode at any moment. Beside him, his twin sister, Adrianna, leaned against his chair, her fingers gripping the leather so tightly her knuckles were white. Her eyes too— same as Lucas's but mirrored—were burning with a quiet rage, her lips pursed tight.

Mika tried to relax in her seat, but it was difficult to say the least. The atmosphere in the room was so tense she could cut it with a knife, the anger from the two Alphas coming off them in waves making it hard to breathe.

Of course, it was understandable. The mages had attempted to kidnap two pups—already considered a grave sin to Lycans as each child was precious—but not just *any* pups. Alessandro Anderson and Diana Corvinus were also future Alphas to two of the most powerful Lycans in the world, born to True Mates, which meant their blood was potent with power. Previously, the mages had tried to kidnap Adrianna and Lucas, hoping to use their blood in whatever ritual they had planned to take over the world. Had the mages succeeded in their attempt tonight, they would have drained both children until there was not a drop of blood left in their fragile bodies.

Beside her, Daric spoke. "Our source called me and told me about his vision. He said that the mages would come for the pups outside Muccino's. I immediately located Mika and brought her to the scene, then proceeded to gather more of our men to help."

Lucas's gaze turned to her. "Why not get our fighters over there first? They were already in the training room. You could have gotten everyone there quicker and then taken Mika after."

A tick in Daric's jaw pulsed. "Our source was specific in his instructions. Take Mika first, and then everyone else."

She turned her head toward him so quickly that a wave of dizziness passed over her. "Me? Why?"

He shrugged. "I don't know. Maybe he saw you saving Sofia first."

"Huh." Yeah, that must be it. If twenty Lycans showed up, it would have been chaos and maybe no one would have thought to help the Lupa first.

Lucas threaded his fingers together and leaned back in his chair. "And then what happened?"

Mika cleared her throat and then proceeded to tell them about everything that happened the moment she arrived on the scene. "....we've found the vans by the FDR, but it seems to be abandoned."

"And what do we know about these men?" Adrianna asked.

"The men who came were trained well, just like the others we've previously encountered," Mika explained.

Adrianna's mismatched eyes flashed with anger. "Hired guns."

"The best," she agreed.

Aside from growing their own numbers, the mages also began to supplement their forces with human fighters, who while not possessing any magic or mystical qualities, had modern weapons and were well-trained. Mika and Daric had initially thought the mages found a way to amplify the power of the necklace of Magus Aurelius so they could control the mind of more than one person at a time. However, as they had discovered in the past year, the mages were simply hiring and recruiting from the best private military contractors around the world to build their army the old-fashioned way—with lots of money. Based on the information and analysis Lizzie had dug up, there was a powerful force behind the mages, one with a seemingly inexhaustible amount of wealth.

"And the pups?" Lucas asked. "Why them?"

"They either want their blood or they want to use them to bargain," Daric said. "Whichever one it is, you know it has something to do with their final plan."

Adrianna rubbed her temple. "We'll have to step up security and keep the pups and Sofia at home as much as possible. And maybe Diana and Alessandro shouldn't be in the same place until we can put a stop to this. It'll make it more difficult for them to spread their efforts."

"I didn't like it when Papa suggested the same thing, but now that I have Alessandro, it makes sense," Lucas said. "But yes, we'll have to tighten our security. Sofia won't like it, but I can't risk her getting kidnapped. I'll talk to Astrid and Nick."

"We'll have our team work on this as soon as possible." Mika stood up. "I'm already having the footage from Muccino's and Petite Louve's security cameras sent to Lizzie. Daric? Can you give me a lift to HQ? I left my car at the cemetery."

Lucas frowned. "The ceme—" His face faltered. "Jesus, Mika, I'm sorry. I forgot what today was."

Adrianna came around toward her, a hand going to her shoulder. "Why don't you go home? It's already ten o'clock You should get some rest."

Despite the tightness in her chest, she managed a shrug. "It's fine." She turned her gaze to Daric. "Let's go."

There was hesitation in his eyes, but she sent him a silent plea to not question her. "Of course."

In the blink of an eye, the Alpha's office disappeared, and they were inside her office at the GI headquarters. With a sigh of relief, she thanked Daric, who only nodded before shimmering away. Walking around to her desk, she booted up her computer and began to type up the events of the evening.

When she first agreed to head the Alpha's anti-mage task force, she didn't think paperwork would be part of the job. But it was imperative she get down the details while they were fresh in her head, as any piece of information could be useful later on. Despite the disturbing events that had happened, she had to stay focused and get to the task at hand.

However, when she got to the part where she was shot and Delacroix helped her by taking her into the shadows, her fingers faltered over the keyboard. How was she supposed to relay what happened, not only how to explain how Delacroix's powers worked, but how she suspected that he might be her True Mate.

Pushing away from the computer, she rose up from her chair. Fatigue seeped into her bones. *Maybe I should go home and get some rest.* Recharge, get up early, come back here and start afresh.

"Oh, crap." Her car was still back at the cemetery. She supposed she would have to take one of the GI cars home for now and then have her car picked up tomorrow. Problem solved, she headed toward the elevators and took one all the way to the garage level. Her mind was so pre-occupied when she stepped out that she collided into someone on the other side.

Damp grass, smoke and—

"You," she hissed, pushing away desire threatening to bubble over inside her. "What are you doing here?"

Dark eyes blinked at her. "Cleanup is done, just headin' home, boss." He cocked his head behind him, where Jacob, Arch, and about a dozen of their guys stood.

Heat bloomed in her cheeks. "Right. Goodnight then." She sidestepped them, and without looking back headed to the row of cars at the other end of the garage, determined to put as much space between them as she could. However, she didn't get very far away when a hand wrapping around her wrist prevented her from taking another step. Electricity bolted up her arm.

"Let me go." When his grip tightened, she turned to face him. "What are you doing?"

"We should talk." The lazy, devil-may-care smile was

gone from his face. Instead, those dark eyes stared back at her with naked desire. "About what happened in—"

"I said. Let. Go!" She yanked her hand away and raced toward the nearest vehicle. The door was barely closed when she punched the ignition button and the engine roared to life, then she put the car into gear and raced out of the garage. Moments later, the car broke through the magical wall that protected the entrance, and she drove as fast as she legally could to The Enclave, a group of buildings on the Upper West Side that the New York clan called home. It was a mini-city, consisting of several apartment buildings where most of the clan lived and protected by many magic spells that made humans ignore it.

She pulled into her spot under her building and cut the engine. Her legs felt like jelly so she didn't dare move yet. Closing her eyes, she rested her forehead on the wheel.

This wasn't fair. Joe was the love of her life. No one else could occupy her heart in that way again. That ... that crude asshole couldn't possibly be her True Mate. She couldn't fall in love with him. If only Joe was still here. Or if only they'd had a baby—

She sat up quickly. True Mates ... if they were True Mates, then that meant he could give her something she'd been wanting—a baby. It wouldn't be Joe's, but it would be *hers*. All hers, to love and care for. Her inner wolf seemed to like the idea of that. A pup to cherish, to fill that void in her heart that had been there since Joe died.

"No, no!" She pushed the door open violently and wrenched herself out of the vehicle, stalking toward the elevators. Crazy. Preposterous. It wasn't like she could ask him to give her a sample—for some reason, IVF couldn't produce any offspring, Lycan or human. No, it would have to be done the old-fashioned way.

And would that be so bad?

"Yes, it would." She jabbed the call button so hard, it would have left a dent were it not made of reinforced steel. "Yes, definitely. Bad idea." Her hormones were raging like a teenager's, but her adult mind knew sex with Delacroix would be a terrible mistake.

And yet ...

A long sigh escaped her, and she stepped into the elevator. Moments later, she finally arrived home. Well, her apartment, anyway. The concept of a home seemed alien to her after she'd sold the house in Brooklyn she had owned with Joe. Though it had been over a year since she'd moved, there hadn't really been time to decorate or even unpack all of her things. There were still two or three boxes in the living room, and all the furniture and decorations had been the same as when she moved in. This place was more like a dorm —she only slept, showered, and dressed here. But then again, her job had taken over her entire life meaning those were the only things she had time for outside of work. Every day melded into the next, same shit, different day.

But maybe a baby would be nice. She could move into a larger place and—

"All right then," she said aloud. "How exactly am I supposed to *ask* him?"

Maybe she didn't have to tell him. From what little information she'd heard, Delacroix had been a major flirt before he left for Zhobghadi. It would be easy enough to seduce him, and then she'd get pregnant. If he was her True Mate, it would only have to happen once.

"Argh!" Her hands curled into fists at her side. No, she couldn't do that. Honesty and integrity were important to her. Besides, tricking a man into getting her pregnant was just so ... icky.

But then again ...

Delacroix was already an amoral bastard. Selfish. Thought only of himself. Oh, she knew that much about him. Nick had told her the entire story, including the fact that Delacroix was planning to go Lone Wolf after his five years of servitude to New York was over. It was obvious he couldn't wait until his sentence was over.

Maybe, just maybe, if she could give him what he wanted, he could give her what she wanted. It would be a fair trade and besides, there was no risk of emotional entanglement, not with him.

Her eyes moved heavenward. Oh Lord, this was insane, right?

CHAPTER FOUR

EVEN THOUGH A FEW DAYS HAD PASSED SINCE THE incident, the strange feeling gnawing at Delacroix didn't go away, and he had a feeling it wasn't going to any time soon. His wolf too, was restless, as if it wanted *something*.

He knew exactly what it wanted. From the moment it laid eyes on her, it wouldn't stop hounding him. Wanting to see her. Smell her delicious, distinct scent—lavender and spice. Thinking about her made his cock twitch.

The sound of a body slamming on the ground jolted him out of his thoughts. His mind suddenly remembered where they were—in the training gym, surrounded by at least twenty other Lycans. Thank the Lord for small favors that his thoughts had been interrupted before they became too salacious.

"Martinez!" a harsh voice growled. "I keep telling you to watch your left side, it's your weakness. Now get up off your ass and try it again."

The young recruit got to his feet. "Sir, yes, sir!"

"This ain't the army, Martinez," said Cliff Forrest, the

head combat trainer for the Guardian Initiative. Forrest was the tallest and largest man Delacroix had ever seen, aside from Prince Karim, which was probably why he'd had a successful career as an MMA fighter. However, it was cut short about a year ago when he'd disappeared from the fighting circuit. There were rumors flying about, something that had to do with a dirty fight, but it was obvious he had decided to use his gifts to help with the fight against the mages. The bastard was tough on his guys, but he had to be, training these men and women for life and death situations.

"How about we make this more interesting?" Forrest's eyes zeroed in on Delacroix and Jacob. "Let's see if Martinez can remember his training under a little more pressure."

Martinez groaned but got into a fighting stance anyway. "Fine."

Delacroix got up from the mat. *"Allons, mon ami."* He offered his hand to Jacob, who took it. They made their way to the center of the mats, and proceeded to pummel Martinez with everything they had. To his credit, the other Lycan fought well and didn't leave his left side open. Once Forrest was satisfied with his performance, he stopped the exercise and dismissed them for their lunch break.

Training with the other recruits wasn't much different from what he and Jacob used to do back in Zhobghadi. In fact, if he were to live the rest of his time, here, doing this, it wouldn't be so bad. But fighting the other night ... the blood and screams had brought back too many memories. And then, when he saw Mika hurt, it nearly drove him insane. There was that urge inside him, one that propelled him forward to take her to safety, to the only place he knew she would truly be safe.

And that's where it all changed.

When she walked into the office that morning, both he and his wolf had taken notice of her. Mika Westbrooke was an attractive woman, and he wasn't blind. But her acrimonious manner had turned him off, even if his wolf didn't care.

But when he took her into the shadow, it was like she turned into the brightest star in the universe. A glow surrounded her, filling the darkness with her light. And that scent. Lord, that scent of lavender and spice haunted his every waking moment since then, as well as the feel of her plush body against his. He didn't want to let her go, but then she scampered away from him the moment they left the shadow, and he hadn't seen her since.

It wasn't that she wasn't coming to HQ. Oh no. She was there, somewhere. That scent of hers lingered in the air, and he could follow her path from the garage to the elevator, sometimes even leaving traces in the cafeteria and the central operations room. But he'd never seen her. It was as if she purposefully avoided him, coming and going only during the times she knew he'd be occupied with training or other duties.

Of course, when he couldn't find a way to bump into her, he tried to get up to the command floor, to where her office was located. But the stupid elevator computer kept telling him "access denied" when he tried to take it up there. No amount of pleading, cursing, or pounding on the controls would make it change its mind. *Access denied, indeed.*

There was a way up there, he knew it. The urge was getting stronger, and his wolf was on the edge. Was she all right? Was she breathing? Did she hate him? He was acting like a *couillion*—a crazy person. But how was he going to know all these things if he couldn't even see her.

"Lizzie just sent me a message. She had Chinese food delivered for lunch," Jacob said as they walked into the locker rooms. "Want some?"

"*Eh*, why not?" The food at the cafeteria was decent, but after living here for a week, he was beginning to get tired of it. "I hope she ordered enough. I'm starving."

The other Lycan snorted. "She wouldn't have invited us if she didn't. Eats more than I do. Let's go before she finishes it all."

Soon they found themselves at the central command floor outside Lizzie's office. Delacroix knocked on the door before poking his head inside. "Oh good, he's not here."

"Who's not here?" Lizzie didn't even look up from her computer screen, face scrunched up in serious concentration as her fingers flew across the keyboard with loud *clickety-clacks*.

"Er, no one." *Your boyfriend*, he said to himself at the same time. Well, Wyatt Creed *could* be her boyfriend if he ever grew some *couilles* and just admitted his attraction to her. Instead, the man acted like a crazy stalker, lurking outside her office and glaring and growling at any man who looked at her in the cafeteria during lunchtime. Lizzie could put him out of his misery by either going out with him or telling him to take a hike, but the female seemed oblivious to the man's attentions. Or any man's, for that matter, as she seemed only interested in her job and her computers.

"Ugh, when does the food get here?" Jacob grumbled as he filed in from behind. He plonked himself on the nearest chair and propped his feet on top of her desk.

"It's on the—" Her face suddenly changed, and she bounded up from her chair. "Oh, food's here!"

"Huh?" How did she know? "I didn't hear a—"

A sharp ring pierced the air, and she pulled a phone from her pocket and spoke into it. "Yeah, send it up please."

"Finally," Jacob groaned. "I'm starving."

With a disgusted sound, she pushed Jacob's booted feet off the table. "I told you to stop doing that, runt."

He stuck his tongue out at her. "And I told you to stop calling me that."

They proceeded to call each other names and hurl creative insults at each other, which he watched with amusement. By now, he had gotten used to the siblings' squabbles. On the outside, it may seem like they hated each other, but it was the opposite. Really, it was one of the ways they showed they cared. Some people used gifts or affirmation as a love language; Jacob and Lizzie used bickering.

"Now, now, children, please stop fighting, at least until after we finish eating." He gave them a mock exasperated sigh. "By the way, thanks for inviting me, Lizzie," he said as he sat opposite from Jacob.

The redhead parked her hip on the side of her desk and pulled a lollipop from her front shirt pocket. "I had an ulterior motive inviting you here." She unwrapped the sucker and popped it into her mouth.

"Really?"

"When you arrived here, I immediately started looking into your background. And you know what I found?"

Now, this was interesting. "What did you find?"

"Absolutely nothing." She pulled the lollipop from her

mouth and waved it around. "Zip. Zilch. Nada. Everyone these days leaves some kind of digital trace. You seem to be a ghost. Now"—she leaned down and poked him in the chest —"how is that possible?"

"Perhaps you're not as good as you think you are," he challenged.

"Uh-oh." Jacob shook his head. "You shouldn't have done that. Now she won't stop."

Lizzie ignored her brother. "Of course I'm good. I'm the best. Even without my powers."

Of course, she was a hybrid too, like her brother. "What are you going to do to me, then? Set my hair on fire?"

"Puh-lease." She waved a hand dismissively. "As if I were so pedestrian."

"Hey!" Jacob protested.

"Admit it, runt, my powers are much more elegant."

"Talking to computers isn't as cool as this." Jacob snapped his fingers, and a small flame shot up from his hand. "What are you gonna do when someone attacks you? Throw a hard drive at them?"

"Wait a minute." His gaze ping-ponged from one sibling to another. "What do you mean *talk to computers?*" Now his curiosity was piqued.

"She talks to them and tells them what to do," Jacob offered. "And they talk back to her."

"But isn't that what a computer essentially does? Communicate?"

"Oh, you poor thing." Lizzie sighed. "Anyone can use a keyboard or mouse or touchpad to tell a computer what commands to execute. What I do is so much more than that." She made a grab at Jacob and swiped the phone from his hand. Ignoring his protests, she held it up and closed her eyes. A moment later, she let go of the device as if it was on fire. "Ew, gross! You're disgusting, Jacob. I can't believe you would watch that! What would Mom say?"

"Ha!" He picked up the phone from the floor and slipped it into the back pocket of his jeans, then fished out another phone from the inside of his jacket. "That was my dummy phone for when you try to snoop into my business. Do you think I'm an amateur? That I haven't learned to keep a fake phone growing up around a technopath?"

A technopath. He'd never heard of such a power. Of course, he didn't know many others who had powers, for that matter. "So, you can communicate with any computer and tell it what to do, just by touching it?"

"I don't even have to be touching it, as long as I was connected to its network," she said with a smug smile.

Interesting. "So, it must bother you then that you couldn't find any information on me."

Lizzie's pert nose wrinkled. "Yes, but I'm also interested on how you managed to cover your digital tracks." Wide blue eyes looked at him with manufactured guilelessness that almost made him snort. "If you could tell me, I would be grateful. It's for you know ... research."

Hmmm, so little miss technopath needed info from me? Maybe he could use this to his advantage. "I could tell you, if you give me something in return."

"What do you—" Lizzie recoiled, her face turning an alarming shade of red. "You pervert. I'm not going to sleep with you."

"What the fuck?" Jacob lifted both hands, flames bursting from his fingers. "I told you if you ever tried—"

"Whoa, whoa, *mes amis*!" It didn't even occur to him that *that* was what she would think. "I'm not talking about that." He shuddered with disgust. Since arriving here, he had come to think of Lizzie as a sister. "I need something else."

Lizzie placed her hands on her hips. "And what would that be?"

"I want you to help me access the elevator computer so I can get anywhere in the building."

Jacob plopped himself back on the chair. "Oh, is that all? Why didn't you say so?"

"*Pshaw*." Lizzie waved her hand dismissively. "I can get around that easily. Why do you need access?"

"And why do you *really* need to know how I covered my tracks?"

She smirked at him. "Fine." There was a knock on the door, and she yelled, "Come in!"

One of the young Lycan analysts walked in holding two large brown paper bags with "Emerald Dragon" printed on the side. The smell of fried rice, spicy chicken, and fragrant beef wafted in the air. Lizzie took the bags from him. "Thanks, Dan, you're such a sweetheart."

Dan blushed furiously. "Anytime, Miss Martin. If you need anything else ..."

"I'll give you call. See ya."

Effectively dismissed, he left the office. She raised the bags. "Before we get down to business, let's eat."

———

After finishing their massive meal, Lizzie agreed to meet Delacroix by the elevators at seven o'clock that evening.

Before going to meet her, he made sure to check that Mika's car was still in the garage. As he'd observed in the last couple of days, she would usually leave early when he had afternoon training, and she left later in the evening during the time he would man the security booth while their usual guard was on dinner break. Tonight, however, he swapped with Jacob without telling anyone else.

She thought she was being sneaky, but he was sneakier.

"All right, I'm here," Lizzie announced as she bounded up to him.

"How long will this take?"

She smirked at him, then pressed her palm against the control panel by the door. "There."

"There?"

The door slid open, and she pointed at the car. "You now have free, unfettered access to go wherever you please." Her gaze narrowed, and she thrust a finger at his face. "Don't make me regret this."

"Never, *ma chouchoutte.*"

"I'm gonna Google what that means later."

He walked into the elevator car and faced the infuriating computer. But this time, when he pressed his palm to the biometric reader and selected the floor to the command room, it replied with "access granted." He grinned at her. "You're a genius, Lizzie."

"Thank you." She shoved her hand between the metal doors as they were closing. "Wait! You haven't told me how you managed to cover your digital tracks. Did you use a YRV64 encryption key? The Descartian-Gogol algorithm with a 865-bit modal frequency? Or was it a—"

He laughed. "*Non.* None of those things."

"Really? Then what?"

She was probably going to hate him, but a deal was a deal. "No one can find information on you if it does not exist."

"I—what?" Her brows knitted. "What do you mean?"

"My former clan lived off the grid, and members were under strict orders to keep digital activities to a minimum. We didn't have internet connection in the bayou, and I've never owned a laptop, PC, or even sent an email." Clan members kept a regular cellphone that could only call or text, but that was it. He had gotten so used to it, he didn't bother trying to change his ways since he'd gotten this far without any of those things.

It took a while to dawn on her, but she finally understood. "Hey, that's not fair!"

"You asked, I answered, *ma chouchoutte*," he said before the elevator doors closed in front of her infuriated face.

As the elevator began to ascend, his inner wolf grew antsy, pacing impatiently. Truth be told, he was too. Maybe this was a mistake. Surely no one else would dare to hack into the elevator system and barge into the upper offices. He could be punished for that, but right now, he just couldn't think about the consequences. That force compelling him to see her would surely drive him mad if he didn't give in.

Luck was on his side as he reached the top floor, the place empty and dark. However, there was one source of light in the entire space—a large corner office with glass windows. He didn't need to be psychic to know it was her, burning the midnight oil. How would she react to his presence here? Well, it was time to find out.

Not even bothering to knock, he walked right into her

office. "It's getting late, *cher*, you should get home and rest, *non*?"

Her head whipped toward him, and her expression changing from surprise to shock and then anger. "What the hell are you doing here?" She bolted to her feet and walked toward him. "And how did you get up here?"

"I have my ways." He stepped forward, moving close enough to get a whiff of her delicious scent. "Now, I think we need to talk."

"I think you need to leave." Her voice took on a deadly edge. "Or you'll regret it."

"You've been avoiding me." When she tried to sidestep him, he merely blocked her way. "Why?"

"Excuse me? Avoiding you? I'm up to my eyeballs in work and—"

"Don't lie, *cher*." He caught her chin and tipped her head up. Defiant emerald eyes shot up to meet his gaze. "Something happened back there. When we were in the shadows. It was like ... you were glowing."

"I don't know what you're talking about. You're the one with powers, you tell me what's going on."

"I can tell you one thing." His finger traced a path from her chin, down her neck, to her collarbone. "No one I've taken into the shadows has done that. Or made me feel this way."

She shivered, but didn't move an inch. "I don't—"

"I said, don't lie to me. What happened back there?"

Her nostrils flared.

"You know, don't you?" His wolf urged him on, scratching at him and growling at him to ... what? "Why do I want you so bad? I can't think about anything else but you.

To take you. Possess you. I need to know." The words spilled out of his mouth so fast, he couldn't stop them. But it was true, all true.

She swallowed and turned her face away. "You can't *un-*know if I tell you."

Her words sounded like a warning. Maybe he *should* back off. But he was never good at taking heed of warnings. "What is it?"

"I ... you understand that this doesn't change anything?"

His patience was running short. "Just *tell* me."

"I ... I think we're ... True Mates."

"What?"

A line appeared between her knitted brows. "You—you don't know anything about True Mates?"

"Should I?"

Her head cocked sideways. "No one in your clan told you?"

Ha. As if Remy took his time to educate his Lycans on anything except what he needed them for. "Why don't you tell me then?"

She took a deep breath. "I need some ... please ... just move away ..." Her hands hovered over his chest, like she was afraid to touch him.

Obligingly, he stepped back. "Now talk."

"Lycans supposedly ... I mean, some of us have that one mate they're meant for. Some call it magic, or fate, and others think it's science and evolution. A survival instinct to ensure the continuation of our race because ..." She took a deep breath. "I'm getting ahead of myself. Well, let's just say that we could be True Mates."

"Like ... soul mates?"

Her face scrunched up distastefully, a move that sent a painful stab to his heart for some reason. "No, I ... it just means we're biologically compatible."

"And how do you know this?"

"There are signs ... see ..." She hugged herself, her hands scrubbing down her arms. "My parents were True Mates, as well as the former Alpha—he's my uncle—and his mate. I've heard it all my life, what they felt when they met."

"And that is ..."

"Your scent ... it smells so good to me. And then, when we touched, there was that spark of electricity."

Her words sent him into shock. So, she had felt it too.

"And my wolf, she ... it's like she ..."

A tightness in his chest coiled up like a spring as he recognized each and every one of the things she said. "You caught mine's attention the moment you walked into the room," he finished.

Her face went pale, and her head bobbed.

"And now it won't stop hounding me." He gritted his teeth. "It wants to be around you all the time and make sure you're safe."

Her voice was barely a whisper. "Mine too."

"But ..." No, he couldn't believe it. It couldn't be. "Am I supposed to do anything? Do we have to get married?"

"No!" The horror in her voice sent another stab of unknown pain through him. "I mean, it's not a requirement or anything. For us to ..."

That should have made him feel relieved. Instead it made him feel something he shouldn't. Had no right to be feeling. "I can't stay here. I won't."

"I know."

Dread filled him. "What do you mean, you *know?*"

"Nick told me everything. He had to, before I agreed to take you on." She blew out a breath. "Xavier's been causing him trouble since he was just a kid. I wasn't really surprised to hear that he'd snuck out of his latest boarding school to go to Mardi Gras." Green emerald pools fixed on him. "And you saved his life."

"I was at the right place at the right time." Actually, he'd been on one of the "errands" his former Alpha had sent him on to a biker bar in New Orleans. That's where he saw the younger Vrost, who had the bad luck—or perhaps it was his lack of common sense—of pissing off the local MC chapter by hustling them at pool. He won fair and square, but the president didn't like being made a fool of, so he had Vrost drugged, and then sent his guys to mess him up. The bikers were about to cart him off to God knows where when Delacroix intervened. "I didn't really think he was in danger."

"That's not how Nick put it. He said those guys put so many drugs in his system, he would have died if he wasn't a Lycan. You took him away to safety with your little trick and then called Nick."

What choice did he have? The boy was unconscious, and the only thing he had on him was a phone. There had already been several missed messages from his father at that point. Of course, when he realized who Nick Vrost was ... well, at that time, he thought it had been good luck. Little did he know that the only way Vrost could get him free of Remy was to transfer him to New York. But he was desperate that night he contacted Vrost, and by then, he had no choice. It was either stay and follow orders, join New York, or go Lone Wolf, which he had not been prepared to do. He could only choose the lesser evil.

"Nick owed you for what you did for Xavier," she finished. "And you didn't waste any time calling in that favor."

"Yes." That was the *short* version anyway. "Vrost and his Alpha had friends in high places. He owed me, why shouldn't I use that?" He was free from Remy's influence, and that was all that mattered. "Fuck," he muttered. How did they get to talking about his history? "You're good at changing the subject. So, this is why you've been avoiding me? Because you didn't want me to find out we were supposedly True Mates."

There was a long pause before she answered. "Yes. I ... not exactly."

"Not exactly? Were you just going to leave me hanging without any explanation as to what was happening? Or avoid me forever?"

"I ... you see." She blew out a breath and muttered something under her breath. "This wasn't ... I was going to ..." Her hands curled at her sides, and her teeth clenched. "I wanted to talk to you about something. To offer you ... a way out. I just didn't know how to go about it."

"A way out?" he echoed again. This was frustrating, the way she talked in half sentences and riddles.

"You see, I wanted to ask you to ... this wasn't ... I was going to—"

"*Cher*, just spit it out."

"I want you to give me something."

"What?"

"A baby."

Something short-circuited in his brain. Surely, he heard wrong. "*Excuse me?*"

Her cheeks turned bright red. "You heard me. I want ... I want a pup."

"With me?"

"Y-yes."

His wolf howled in agreement. But him ... "Surely I'm not your top candidate." This was a joke, right?

"You're not," she bit out. "But my she-wolf thinks you're our True Mate, so I don't have a choice. You're the only one who could give me a pup."

He scratched his head. "I'm not an educated man, hell I didn't even finish high school, but I'm pretty sure I know how biology works."

"Not True Mate biology," she said. "You see, if we ... if we ... you and I ..."

"Fucked," he completed.

Her lips pursed distastefully. "Yes. If we did, then I'll get pregnant right away. We don't even have to do it more than once."

He stared at her, still waiting for the punchline. When she remained silent, he knew she wasn't joking. "You're serious."

"I am."

There was something in her voice ... a quiet desperation. So, she wanted a baby so bad that even he would do?

"I could give you something too," she added. "Something you want."

His jaw tensed. "And you know what I want?"

"You want freedom," she stated. "I can help you."

A sardonic laugh escaped his lips. "You can get the Alpha

to free me from my sentence? I doubt even you have that power. Vrost was very clear on that."

"I can get you out of GI," she said. "You could get a cushy job guarding the Alpha or his family. It's what you wanted, right? What you thought you were signing up for?"

That's what Vrost had initially told him. That he would be part of the training group for the Lycan Security Force, and he would be spending the rest of his time here standing in the background looking tough or opening limo doors. Compared to what Remy had him doing all his life, it sounded like a vacation. "So, you could have me transferred?"

"Yes. And who knows? If Lucas likes you enough, he could shorten your service." She huffed. "I'm sure someone like you could make that work."

"Someone like me? You mean an opportunist."

She crossed her arms over her chest. "If it walks like a duck ..."

So that's what she thought of him? She'd already made up her mind that he was a selfish prick, but a prick she could use. "You obviously don't have a good opinion of me, but you're willing to let me fuck you."

"I told you what I want," she said. "And what I can give you. It's up to you to accept or not."

"I wouldn't make a good father." *Jesu*. Him? No, it was a bad idea. He didn't have a clue how to be a father.

She snorted. "I don't need you to be there for that."

"So, I would get you knocked up and just conveniently disappear?"

"Sounds like every guy's dream," she shot back.

"You have a high opinion of yourself, if you think that way." The words flew out before he could stop them, but he couldn't help it. Hurt flashed across her face for just a second, but it was enough for his wolf to slash his insides in anger. Not that he needed the reminder that he was a bastard for saying that. "You could be wrong. Are you willing to test the theory that we are True Mates?"

She ground her teeth. "To get what I want, I'd do anything. Surely you can understand that."

He did, but ... a child?

"I'd take care of everything," she added. "You wouldn't have to do anything. In fact, I'd prefer it if you weren't in the pup's life. Or mine. I don't want or need a relationship, so I'm not going to trap you into anything or ask for child support. I won't tell anyone you're the father. It would be the perfect arrangement. You get what you want, and I get what I want."

She was right. His brain was telling him to take the bargain. It was the perfect arrangement, and he wouldn't have to fight anymore. Not to mention, he could finally get her out of his system by having sex with her. His body, too, was telling him yes. "I don't think so."

"What?" She looked truly surprised, like it hadn't occurred that he would say no.

"I said ... no." Lord, why was it hard to say that one little word?

"Oh." She straightened her shoulders, then walked around to her desk before sitting down. "All right then."

That was it? She asked him for pup, and when he said no, she was just dismissing him? "What are you going to do now?"

"Does it matter?" She didn't even bother looking up at him. "You know your way out."

Her curt dismissal stung like a hundred paper cuts, and

he could only nod and turn on his heel, then stalk out of the office.

His wolf growled at him, unable to understand what happened, only caring that he was walking away from *her*. He couldn't explain it to the animal; *merde*, he couldn't even begin to process it himself, what just happened. All he knew was that the emotions inside would explode if he didn't get out of here, and if that happened, he didn't know what he would do. He needed to get away now before he marched back in there and told her he'd changed his mind.

CHAPTER FIVE

DELACROIX TOLD HIMSELF THAT HE HAD MADE THE right decision. That she would offer up such a bargain was preposterous anyway. He'd never even dreamed of having children himself; the truth was, he hadn't thought he'd make it past the age of twenty, as the "errands" Remy sent him on became more and more dangerous. To bring a child into the world ...

But then again, there was another voice inside him asking, *so what?* Mika was a capable woman and would surely love and spoil any child of hers. It wouldn't be an irresponsible decision. With his past indiscretions, he could have gotten any woman pregnant and none of them would have been half the mother she could be. And then there was the thought of fucking her. Being deep inside her, and driving into—

Immediately, he put a stop to those thoughts. *Merde,* was he really thinking about this? He hit his forehead on the table.

"Yo, D, everything okay?" Jacob cocked his head at him

from where he sat across the cafeteria table. "Dude, did you sleep at all last night?"

How could he sleep these past two nights? Any spare moment he had were plagued with thoughts of Mika, wondering what her lips tasted like or how soft the skin would be between her thighs. And when he did manage to get any sleep, all he did was dream of her. That scent haunted him, even while he was dreaming, and it was driving him crazy. "I'm fine," he snapped. "Just tired."

Jacob raised his palms in the air. "All right, no need to bite my head off. Sheesh."

He pushed his tray away, not really feeling hungry. "Have you ever heard about True Mates?"

"Yeah. Sure. My parents are True Mates," he said nonchalantly.

"And ..."

"And?"

He needed to know, and Jacob was possible the only person he could ask. "Do they really ... is it true that they just need to do it once and—"

"Ew, gross!" He made a gagging sound. "I do *not* want to think about my parents having sex."

"I wasn't asking about *them*," he sighed. "I mean, is there really such a thing?"

Jacob stared at him; his mouth open. "Are you serious right now? You've never heard of them?"

"*Non.*"

"Well, here's what I know."

As Jacob proceeded to tell him pretty much what Mika had told him about True Mates, he listened intently.

"....and that's just about what I know. I'm not really into this shit."

"So True Mates don't even have to be both Lycans?"

"No. Look at Deedee and Karim."

"The king and queen are True Mates?" Why did he not know this? "But no one's ever said anything before."

"I dunno. Maybe you weren't listening. How do you think she got knocked up so quick?" Jacob pointed to his roast beef sandwich. "Are you going to eat that?"

"Go ahead."

So, she was telling the truth, at least about the existence of True Mates. But that didn't mean he and Mika were such a pairing.

His wolf let out a low growl of disagreement.

Oh, what do you know?

"So," Jacob began as soon as he finished gobbling up the sandwich. "We've got the night off tonight. Whaddaya say we go for dinner at *Petite Louve* and then head to Blood Moon? A couple of other guys are going."

It had been a while since he'd had a nice meal. He'd been to the French restaurant before, and the chef was Lycan. "Why not?" And then afterwards ... well maybe he'd get lucky at Blood Moon. The club was the place to be for Lycans, and on a Friday night like this, it would be packed. A little friendly female company wouldn't be bad, help him forget all this business about True Mates.

His wolf yowled at him again, obviously displeased at his thoughts.

Shut up.

———

"That was delicious," Jacob said as he polished off his steak and took a swig of wine.

"I agree." Delacroix's mood lifted considerably as soon as they left HQ. He'd been cooped up there for too long, and a night out was exactly what he needed.

His wolf, on the other hand, was still a miserable bastard, whining and clawing at him, but he ignored it. Tonight, he was going to have some fun, and no one, not even the animal he shared his body with, was going to ruin it.

"God, I can't wait to get to Blood Moon," said Jack Moore, a GI agent who Delacroix remembered as one of his fellow trainees from the Lycan Security Force last year. He quite liked the guy, as he was affable and always willing to lend a hand. "Last week, I met this blonde there who was smokin' hot. Not to mention smart. Works at Fenrir's legal department. We went to her place, and she kept me up all night long."

"Can't be too smart if she took ya home," quipped Tony Buzzio, a wisecracking Lycan who grew up in Jersey. New York and New Jersey were tightly allied, so it made sense that there were a few Lycans from that clan who joined GI.

Jacob called for the check. "It's still a little early. Let's go grab a few drinks at that bar on forty-sixth before we head to Blood Moon."

As soon as they finished paying the bill, the group got up and headed for the exit. Moore grabbed a passing cab, and the first group left. Delacroix flagged the next one that passed them and motioned for everyone to get in. While he waited for his companions to get in, something in his peripheral vision caught his eye.

Thanks to his Lycan vision, he clearly saw Mika sitting in

the restaurant across the street, and she was not alone. Sitting across the candlelit table from her was a man, perhaps a few years older than her, wearing an expensive-looking suit. From the way she leaned forward and smiled at him, it was obvious she knew him well.

"*Feet pue tan.*"

"D?" Jacob asked from the backseat of the cab. "You comin'?"

"I'll catch up." He slammed the door shut without any explanation and stalked across the street. Not wanting her to see him yet, he melted into the shadows, following the path of darkness toward the large glass window.

He stayed hidden, thanks to the shadow cast by the building next door. While he couldn't hear what they were talking about, he could see how familiar and comfortable they were with each other. Every now and then, he would say something that put a wistful look on her face, then reach across the table to cover her hand. It made him sorely want to pummel his face in, and his wolf agreed, letting out a growl loud enough to rattle his chest.

Who the fuck was this man? And what was she doing here with him? If she had a boyfriend in the first place, why come to him with that silly proposition?

Unless this man was—

Fuck!

As their dinner plates were being cleared, Mika stood up, and he knew this was his chance to find out what the hell was going on. Stepping out from the shadows, he marched right into the restaurant. Luckily, the host station was unmanned and so he followed her down a long narrow hallway into the rear of the restaurant, silently slipping into the shadows so she wouldn't detect him. God, she was so sexy as she walked in her stiletto heels. Her little black dress clinging to her hips and ass made him jealous of how close the fabric was to her naked skin. Instead of its customary braid, her long black hair hung in loose waves down her back.

When she reached the end of the hallway, she went into the door on the right marked with the ladies' room sign. The door was about to close but he managed to slip inside, then slammed it shut and locked it behind him.

The loud slam made Mika whip around, her emerald eyes widening with surprise. "What th—"

He grabbed her arms and pressed her up against wall, holding her tight. She struggled, and he gripped her tighter.

"Are you insane? What the hell are you doing in here? Anyone can just walk in."

"I locked the door," he said matter-of-factly. "Who the fuck is that man?"

"Who—you mean, Frank?"

"Is that his name?" *Frank.* Even from his name, he sounded like an asshole. "Who. The fuck. Is he?"

"None of your goddamn business," she hissed. "I can't believe—wait, are you following me?"

"Don't flatter yourself. Now tell me." He pressed up against her, trapping her so she couldn't even move her lower body. "Is he the next guy on your list?"

"On my list?"

"On your sperm donor list," he snarled. "Think a guy like that could knock you up?"

"Fuck you," she spat.

"So that's the problem," he growled as he lowered his head. "But I can fix that."

"Don't you dare, I—*mm!*"

Her protests died under his mouth as he captured her lips. God, she was even sweeter than in his fantasies and dreams. He wanted more of her, urging her to open to him, licking his tongue along the seam of her lips to coax her to open up.

"Stop!" She had pushed him away using all her Lycan strength. "You can't do this."

"I can do what I want."

"Asshole!" She raised her hands, lunging for him, but he caught them and pushed her up against the sink. "Let me go, you bastard. This is my business, and I'll thank you to stay out of it."

"I've changed my mind."

He must have caught her off guard because she relaxed. "Huh?"

"About your proposition. The other night."

"What the—you can't do that."

"I can and I will. But you have to get rid of the other guy. Now."

"Frank?"

"Yes, *Frank.*" Hearing his name on her lips made him want to break something. It made him think of that bastard, between her legs, and her moaning his name. No, his name would be the only thing she would be screaming. "Well, do you agree?"

His heart seemed to stop right up until the moment she nodded. "Fine."

Damn, she must want this baby so bad. "Good. Name the time and place."

She thought for a moment. "Tomorrow, eight o'clock in

the evening. St. James Hotel on the Upper East Side."

"I'll be there." He raked his hand into her hair, pulling her head back. But as he lowered his head again, she twisted away.

"No."

"No?"

"No ... no kissing on the lips."

"What the hell do you mean, no kissing?"

"It's too intimate," she said. "And not necessary for what has to be done."

"And Frank, are you going to kiss him tonight before sending him on his way?"

"Go to hell, Delacroix," she spat out. "It's one of my conditions."

Just one? "Fine, but I have some of my own."

"What are they?"

"I want the entire night."

Her brows knitted together. "What do you mean?"

"According to what I've heard, it only takes one time—the first time—for True Mates to get pregnant. But I don't want a wham bam thank you, sir." His hand skimmed down to her thigh, pulling the skirt up to expose her skin. "Your sweet little body will be mine the entire night. To do with as I please."

"Until midnight."

"Morning," he said. "Or no deal."

"I—fine." She crossed her arms over her chest. "Anything else?"

He was sorely tempted to add more conditions, but he didn't want to piss her off. "None. But I don't want you to forget who you'll belong to." Spinning around, he made her face the mirror, pulling her arms behind her. Fuck, she was gorgeous like this—green eyes blazing with fury at him, hands behind her, pressed up against him, her breasts heaving so hard they could pop out of her dress any time. He pressed his raging erection up against her plush ass.

"What are you doing? I'm not going to have sex with you here, you asshole." Her struggling only made his cock swell even more.

"This is just a preview, *cher*." He lifted the bottom of her dress, and his hand crept up her smooth thigh. His fingers skimmed the fabric of her panties, but instead of recoiling, she sighed, her mouth parting. Encouraged, he slipped his hand under the elastic, feeling her smooth, shaved mound, then down to her nether lips.

"Wet already?" She was soaked. He brushed her clit with his finger, which must have sent her arousal through the roof as her scent intensified. Goddamn, he nearly came in his pants right there.

"Stop ... teasing," she said through gritted teeth as she pushed her hips against his hand.

"Tsk, tsk, so impatient, *cher*." He plunged a finger inside her, making her moan with pleasure as his thumb began to rub her sensitive nub.

"That's it," he encouraged. Her hips moved rhythmically against his hand, and her sweet little pussy sucked his fingers greedily. "Come on now. Be a good girl and come."

She let out a sharp cry, her body tensing like a taut bow before convulsing with short shudders, her pussy tightening around his digits. Her whimper as her pleasure washed over her went straight to his cock, and unable to stop himself, he pushed his erection against her ass, taking only three thrusts before he came, a groan ripping from his throat as pleasure shuddered over him.

Merde, he hadn't done that since he was a teenager. But everything about her was so fucking sexy, she could have made him come by looking at him.

As she stood there limply in his arms, he pulled down her dress. "I'll see you tomorrow, Mika." He reached for a couple of paper towels from the dispenser and cleaned himself up, then nipped her shoulder and rubbed his wrists on her neck before striding out of the bathroom. As soon as he was far enough away, he let out a long breath. It took all his Goddamn control not to go back in there and fuck her against that sink. Patience, he told himself. He'd have her entire sweet body soon, and he could fuck her out of his system. Tomorrow couldn't come soon enough.

CHAPTER SIX

It seemed like a lifetime before Mika lifted her head to look up at her reflection in the mirror. Her hair was mussed, face flushed, and her lipstick smeared. She braced herself on the marble counter or else she would have melted into a puddle on the floor after that powerful orgasm.

Damn that bastard! God, she despised him. After rebuffing her offer, he had the nerve to stalk her and then come in here and tell her he'd changed his mind. And all because he thought—

"Shit." *Frank.* He was still waiting outside. But how could she face him like this? It was a good thing he was human and wouldn't be able to smell Delacroix's scent on her. The asshole rubbed his scent all over her as if marking her. *It was that True Mates instinct*, she told herself. He couldn't help himself. Nothing more.

She righted herself as quick as she could, cleaning up the lipstick and rubbing her body down with paper towels sprayed with perfume. *It would have to do for now.* Her wolf didn't like having the male's scent rubbed away, but, well, *boo-hoo, tough titties.*

Satisfied with the cleanup job, she walked out of the bathroom, and by the time she reached the table, she had stopped wobbling on her heels. "Sorry to take so long, Frank," she said, easing herself back onto her chair, ignoring the delicious soreness between her legs. "I had to take a call. From the office."

"Everything okay?" her dinner companion asked.

She nodded. "Yeah, it's fine. What were we talking about?"

Frank Woods flashed her a bright smile, his handsome face lighting up as he continued his story. Frank had been Joe's best friend since childhood and was his best man at their wedding. The loss had been just as devastating for him as it had been for her, so it was natural they had gravitated toward each other after he died. He'd been her rock throughout the whole thing, and they still got together every now and then. Knowing it had been Joe's birthday two weeks back, he called her to see how she was doing and made plans to have dinner to catch up.

It really was silly Delacroix would think Frank was "on her list." After the Cajun turned down her offer, there was no list. No matter how much it had hurt, she was starting to get used the fact that a child wasn't in her future.

"Are you sure you're all right?" he asked. "You usually love the desserts here."

She looked up from her uneaten tiramisu. "Well, you know. Just things."

His hand reached over and covered hers. "Yeah, I know. But ... we all have to move on."

"We do."

"So, uh, are you seeing anyone?" His expression was ... hopeful?

She wanted to jerk her hand back but resisted the urge. Instead she slid it out of his grasp and patted the top of his hand. "No, I'm not." What would he think of her plan to have a baby? She could only hope he didn't want to put himself forward as a candidate.

An awkward moment passed between them before she spoke. "We should probably leave. I mean, I want to go home."

"Oh." His face faltered. "Of course. It was nice seeing you." He shook his head when she grabbed her purse. "No, let me. Please, you paid the last time."

She smiled weakly. "Okay, if you insist."

After Frank paid the bill, they left the restaurant and went their separate ways. She drove home, trying not to think about tomorrow, but that was impossible. It was even harder as she lay in bed alone with her thoughts and nothing else to occupy her.

Her hand went down to her flat belly. *It's really going to happen.* In twenty-four hours, she could possibly be pregnant. By Delacroix.

Damn him, why did he have to be such a bastard? Of course, she should be glad he was an asshole. It would be easier to forget about him afterwards when they went their separate ways. He would be a terrible father, but an even worse mate. Probably cheat on her the first chance he got. The thought made her want to rip her sheets to shreds. Her wolf, too, wanted to maim and claw those imaginary females, but they had to accept it. After he got her pregnant, he would be having sex with many other women, and she couldn't do or say anything about it.

"Argh!" She flipped over and sank her face into her pillow. *Can't think of that. Just think of the beautiful little pup you'll be holding in your arms in nine months.*

Even her wolf seemed appeased by the thought and lay down quietly.

Yes, in just a few months, she would have everything she wanted, and Delacroix would be out of her life.

———

When she signed up for this job, Mika knew there would be no weekends or vacations. She was all right with that schedule because she had pretty much thrown herself into her work at her previous position at the special investigations unit of the Lycan Security Force. So, even though it was Saturday, she had to come in to her office and plow through a pile of work, plus, she had scheduled an important conference call with a contact abroad.

"....she's not budging on that item. And that's about it."

"Thanks for the update, Julianna."

Her cousin Julianna—formerly Anderson—MacDougal's pretty face was drawn into a frown as it filled the screen of her monitor. "Ivanova's a tough nut to crack, but I'll work on her. I know this alliance with Moscow would help us out a lot." Along with her husband Duncan, she served as envoy to the New York clan, and their main job was to travel around the world meeting with other clans to get them into their fight against the mages. Currently, they were in Moscow, trying to get the current Alpha on their side.

While their kind had to follow rules set by the Lycan High Council, clans all over the world were pretty much independent of each other, unless they had a formal alliance. It was Lucas and his father Grant's idea to get all the Lycan clans together to help fight the mages. Many were eager to join the fight, but some were harder to convince. Julianna and Duncan had been talking with the Moscow Alpha for months, but they kept getting rebuffed when it was time to talk formal alliances.

Mika was getting impatient and wanted the damn thing sorted out. "According to our sources, there's a big surge of power just outside the city on the east side. Cross went there to investigate a couple of times, and he says there's definitely mage activity. He couldn't get too close without blowing his cover, but he says it should be our next target." Unless they had the Alpha's permission, they couldn't just mobilize a force and attack the mage hideout. It was a rule set up long ago to prevent clans from invading or encroaching on another's territory.

Julianna pursed her lips. "Damn. Ivanova's playing hard to get, and I know she wants something but won't tell me."

"It's vital we get her on our side." And she was eager to get this Russian situation behind her. But Natalia Ivanova had been making the negotiations difficult from the very beginning.

"I know. We haven't failed yet, and I'll be damned if I let this one get away." She let out a yawn.

"What time is it there?"

"Too damn late ... or early." A loud wail made her wince. "Sorry."

"Kieran's still not sleeping?" Much like most of the

couples who had found their True Mates, Julianna and Duncan had recently welcomed their first pup, a son. He was only a couple of weeks old but was probably the most well-traveled infant in the world since his parents toted him around wherever they went.

"The kid doesn't seem to have any concept of jet lag. Duncan's with him now, but that cry means he's hungry." Julianna got up from her chair and turned to her right. "Yeah, yeah, hold your horses, Kier! Your milk factory's coming." She let out an exasperated sigh. "I'll talk to you soon, Mika."

"Later, Julianna." The screen went dark, and Mika reached over to turn her monitor and computer off.

She had recognized the tired look on her cousin's face but also saw the happiness behind those weary eyes. To think that while growing up, Julianna always said she didn't want to have babies, but now, she too had found her True Mate and had a pup.

Soon, she told herself. In a few months, she would have a baby of her own to keep her up at night with pooping, peeing, and feeding. And she would have the happiness that eluded her all these years.

She was glad for the work that had to be done today because otherwise, thinking about tonight would have driven her crazy. Or make her lose her nerve. Glancing at the clock, she saw that it was time to leave if she wanted to have time to check into the hotel room before Delacroix arrived at eight. She closed up her office and went down to the garage.

The drive to the hotel was a blur from the moment she got into her car until she handed her keys to the valet. After checking in, she left one set of keys with the front desk in an envelope with Delacroix's name on it. She hadn't thought to get his phone number so she could text him the room number, but she knew he'd be smart enough to figure it out.

Mika had never stayed in this hotel, but she had a friend visit her once who had stayed here. It was the first place that popped into her mind when Delacroix asked her where to meet, and she figured it was as good a place as any. She couldn't very well invite him to her place or go up to his room at HQ. This hotel room was comfortable enough, but also coldly impersonal. Just like what this night would be like.

Anticipation, nervousness, and excitement all swirled in her stomach. She wasn't inexperienced, but it had been so long since she'd last had sex. She attempted the one-night stand thing a few months after Joe died figuring it was time, but aside from a couple of torrid kisses, she couldn't go through with it. It felt like a betrayal at that time.

And now?

She mentally shook her head. No, this wasn't about Joe. Never had been. He was gone. This was about moving on with her life and finally getting what she wanted after her life had been torn apart.

A knock made her startle. Checking the clock, she realized she had been standing there longer than she thought and padded toward the door. She took a breath, knowing that once she opened this door, there would be no turning back.

"Hello, *cher*."

Her heart stopped for three beats when her gaze landed on his handsome face. She swallowed hard as she took in the sight of him dressed so casually in a black T-shirt stretched tight across his wide chest, tapering down to his slim waist. The moment she got a whiff of his scent, her wolf let out a low, longing yowl.

"I didn't have time to get ready."

His eyes moved along her body, and heat pooled in her belly at the lazy admiration. "You look ready enough."

"I mean, I should get showered and dressed." She had planned to at least get cleaned up and change out of her usual office attire of a blouse and pencil skirt and into the little red dress she had brought. Not like she needed to seduce him further, but she thought it would be a good incentive in case he changed his mind.

"Dressing up would seem unnecessary, though I appreciate the thought." He cocked his head to the side. "Aren't you going to let me in?"

Wordlessly, she stepped back and gestured for him to come inside. "Do you want a drink? Or food? I can order—"

"*Non.*" He cleared his throat. "No, thank you. Perhaps we should just skip the preliminaries and—"

"Get this over with?" she snapped, then regretted her words. While she was eager for what would happen after, truthfully, the thought that this was some kind of transaction between them stung. But that was all that it was, right?

"*Cher,*" he began. "If you've changed your mind—"

"I haven't," she stated. "You're right, we should just get it over with." She turned around so he couldn't see her face, but he caught her arm.

"Those were your words, not mine. I want you, Mika," he growled. "And I intend to have you. You're mine. This body"—he ran his hands down to her hips and pulled her ass flush against his hips—"is mine."

"For tonight."

"Until the morning." He was already hard, as evident by the thick bulge pushing up against her ass. God, she'd been imagining his cock since last night when he did the exact same thing and then rubbed himself against her until he came. "I'm going to do whatever I want with this sweet little body. And you'll let me. Do you know why?"

She shook her head, unable to speak.

"Because you'll *want* me to do those things."

A shiver ran through her. Maybe this was a mistake. But her body was singing with need at his words, her pussy growing wet in anticipation. The bastard must have smelled her arousal because he gave a little laugh. "So sweet." He turned her around again and lowered his head.

"No kissing," she warned.

"No kissing *on the lips*, you said." He wrapped her braid around his fist and tugged, pulling her head to the side before pressing his mouth to the pulse at her neck.

"That's not—Oh!" He nipped at her, and pleasure sizzled straight to her core. She tried to push him away, but he wouldn't budge and continued his assault. He mouthed at the sensitive skin of her neck, the soft hairs of his beard tickling her as he switched from kissing to nibbling little bites. His tongue painted soft, sensuous strokes across her nape and shoulders. When his grip on her braid tightened and he tugged hard, she couldn't stop the loud moan that escaped her mouth.

"Please ..."

He continued to kiss her neck and shoulders, and laved her with his mouth and tongue. When he did pull back, she let out a needy whimper.

Without a word, he lifted her and walked them toward the bed. He set her down, making her sit at the edge of the mattress, then knelt between her spread legs. Reaching toward her, he unbuttoned the front of her blouse slowly, parting the fabric to reveal her black lace bra.

He whispered something in French she couldn't understand, then leaned forward to press his hot mouth between her breasts, nuzzling her cleavage with his nose. Reaching up, he shucked the blouse and the straps off her shoulders, freeing her breasts so he could capture a nipple between his teeth.

She hissed at the pleasure–pain and thrust her hands into his hair. Much to her surprise, it was soft at the nape. When she gave a tug, he growled and sucked her nipple harder.

A thrill surged through her knowing she could elicit such a response from him. Hell, if she were honest, the fact that he wanted her so bad was exciting and added to her own pleasure.

You're doing this to get pregnant, her brain reminded her. But she couldn't bring herself to care anymore.

His other hand slid up her thighs and under her skirt. Oh God, just having his fingers near her pussy again was enough to soak her panties. Nudging her thighs farther apart, his fingers sought the damp fabric pushing it aside to touch her wet lips. The digits teased her, moving up and down her slit and barely missing her clit. She ground her hips forward, seeking that pleasure he had given her last night and more.

"So impatient, *cher,*" he murmured against her breast. "I told you you'll want it."

"Fuck you," she spat. "I—"

A hand reached up to collar her throat, and *Goddammit,* that act of dominance made her want him even more.

"Don't be ashamed, Mika." He loosened his hold on her neck, but his other hand continued its ministrations between her legs. "It's just you and me here." He slipped a finger inside her. "I've been dreaming of your pussy since last night." Another finger joined in, and he began to move his hand back and forth. "*Merde,* I've been dreaming of it since I met you."

She let out a strangled moan as his thumb brushed her clit, strumming it so expertly that her body tightened as it prepared for her orgasm.

"That's it," he encouraged. "Come for me. You look so beautiful when you come."

Crying out, she grabbed his shoulders, digging into them with her fingers as a powerful orgasm rocked her body. He continued cooing to her in English and French, his hand working her until the waves of pleasure ebbed away, leaving her body limp.

"Good girl." He withdrew his hand, then popped his fingers into his mouth. "I'll get a taste of you later. But for now ..." Standing up, he towered over her.

Her brows knitted together as she looked up at him, confused.

"Come now, you don't expect me to do all the work, *non?*"

The smug shit. "Of course not." She supposed he was right, but maybe she could have some fun too. That tiny thrill she got when he reacted to her was just a taste, but oh so heady that she could get drunk on it.

Reaching for the bottom of his shirt, she rose and dragged it up, exposing his perfect six-pack abs. Damn, she wanted to bite them. *Maybe later.* For now, she continued to pull the shirt up, dragging it over his head with his help, and then tossed it aside. Her greedy eyes soaked in his naked chest, following the swirls of ink that dragged across his golden tanned skin, her fingers following in her gaze's wake. When her thumb brushed a nipple and made him groan, a surge of lust gripped her, and she leaned forward and pressed the flat of her tongue against his nipple.

"Mika ..." His entire body tensed, and she continued to tease him, her mouth moving lower, over his rock-hard abs. Her teeth grazed over his skin, and he let out a hiss.

Fuck, he was hot. She'd been around Lycans all her life and seen them in various states of undress, so it was nothing new to her. But Delacroix was an exceptional specimen, and at the very least, she acknowledged that she was lucky that he was attractive and sexy. No wonder all those women wanted him. The thought of him having sex with other women made an unreasonable jealousy rise inside—

"Uh, *cher*?" He looked down at her expectantly.

Right. There was a task *at hand.* She smirked up at him as she tugged on the fly of his jeans. One by one, she popped the buttons, then pulled them down along with his boxers.

Oh, mercy me.

He was already rock-hard, his cock thick and long and bobbing up and down as if promising her a good fucking. Jesus, maybe she shouldn't have waited so long to have sex again. It would have been uncomfortable even if she hadn't been celibate for over two years.

Well, this is what I signed up for. Tentatively, she wrapped her fingers around the shaft, feeling its weight and girth in her hands. He jerked at her touch, a strangled cry coming from his throat as she began to move her hand over him, stroking him, feeling the pulse of his cock.

"*Jesu*," he moaned, thrusting his hips forward. It only

encouraged her, and she gripped him tighter as her strokes quickened. "I ... stop." He grabbed her hand and pulled it away with a groan. "Sorry, *cher*. I can't ... it's been too long."

Before she could ask him what he meant, Delacroix had hauled her up and pushed her back on the bed. She scrambled back as he shrugged his pants and underwear from his ankles, along with his shoes. He reached for her and tugged at her skirt, trying to find the zipper but gave up in two seconds and ripped it down the middle before doing the same to her panties.

"Hey!" she cried, but damn, it was fucking hot.

"Sorry ... can't wait to taste you."

"What?"

The ripped fabric was cast aside as his head dove between her legs, his mouth pressing against her soaked lips. His tongue lapped at her, licking and sucking until she was moaning and clutching at the sheets. But he didn't stop, and he continued to tease her, drinking up her juices and flicking her clit with his tongue until she was shuddering with another orgasm.

"God ... Marc ... I ..."

Her heart pounded as he crawled over her like a looming shadow. Her legs spread to accommodate him, his weight pressing on top of her deliciously. He braced himself on one elbow and reached down between their bodies with his other hand.

She sucked in a breath as she felt his blunt tip against her entrance. He pushed forward, and despite her wetness, there was still a slight burning as he fully seated in her. He looked down at her, and when she tried to turn her head away from him, he thrust his fingers into her hair and tugged at her scalp. Her gaze lowered.

"Look at me."

Unable to disobey him, she did, slowly, until she met his dark, lust-fueled eyes. They were so magnetic that she couldn't turn away even as he began to thrust inside her. Deeper, harder, faster. Her hips moved up to meet his in a frantic motion. Heat flushed on her cheeks as he continued to watch her as he was deep inside her.

He rocked into her with a frenetic rhythm that was making her core tighten. She dug her heels into his lower back, trying to take him deeper. Her toes curled as she cried out, bowing her spine off the mattress, and her pussy fluttered around him. He groaned and broke her gaze, bending down to kiss and lick at her neck, moving down to suck on her nipples as he continued to fuck into her, moving with an incessant energy that seemed limitless.

Her greedy little pussy wanted more of him, tightening around him as he thrust over and over again. He looked up at her again, his face tight, but those dark eyes just as stormy. A snarl escaped his mouth, and he pummeled faster, slamming into her hips with such force that it shook the bed.

Her stomach clenched again, the tightness spreading out over her entire body. He must have sensed her impending orgasm because he kept up his pace relentlessly. She reached up to grab his shoulders, and her nails dug deep as pleasure tore through her body, and he let out a long, low grunt. His hands clamped around her hips to steady her, thrusting his pelvis tight as his cock pulsed inside her, flooding her with his seed as he came before collapsing on top of her.

When the roaring in her ears stopped, she opened her

eyes. Her vision returned to normal as did the feeling in her body. She gave herself another minute to recover and catch her breath, but her limbs felt too weak to even try to move.

Fuck, that was amazing. She couldn't deny that, no matter how she tried. Did he enjoy it as much as she did? Did he want to stay until morning as he said, or would he leave now that the job was done?

He stirred, pulled away from her and fell to the mattress next to her. "I promise it will be longer the next time."

Next time. And longer? It had felt like forever. But at the same time, over too soon. "What are you—" An arm wrapped around her waist and rolled her to her side, then pulled her against him. "Are you trying to cuddle?" She wiggled, but his grip was like a vice. Then she heard a soft snore. "Delacroix?" Nothing. "Marc?" With a long sigh, she relaxed against him.

Exhaustion was ready to take over as her lids became heavy. But before she gave in to sleep, she couldn't help but smile as her hand crept down to her belly. Everything that had happened to her up until this point would have been worth it when she held her baby in her arms. Plus, her plans had already been set in motion, even before she came here tonight. She got what she wanted, and now, she had to fulfill her end of the bargain.

She would worry about any consequences another time.

CHAPTER SEVEN

DESPITE HAVING AN ENTIRE NIGHT TO ENJOY HER BODY, the need inside him didn't abate. He took her on the bed, in the shower, and even pressed up against the glass window of the hotel room, but it didn't seem enough. Only exhaustion kept him from reaching for her again after the last time. The clock read five o'clock by the time Delacroix gave in to sleep, rolling away from Mika, their bodies sticky with sweat as their scents mingled on the sheets.

As soon as the fog cleared from his mind when he woke up, his arm stretched across the bed, searching for her warm body. When his hand felt only cool sheets, he opened his eyes.

"Mika?"

He sat up, rubbing his hand down his face. The clock now flashed eight thirty. Rolling off the bed, he stalked to the window and pulled the blackout curtains apart, his eyes shutting as the light temporarily blinded him. When he regained his sight, he glanced around and realized the room was empty and silent. She wasn't buried under the covers, and his sensitive hearing could only detect silence from bathroom. Her scent was faint in the air, and he knew she had been gone a while.

Fury coiled in his chest. *Coward.* She just left him without saying goodbye. Usually, he was the one sneaking out in the morning—and sometimes, he didn't even wait until then. Now the shoe was on the other foot, as they say, and he found he didn't like it.

But this was their deal, right? She was his for one night. He wanted to be angry at her but found he couldn't. His wolf, too, whined pathetically, sniffing the air to soak in her trace scent. *Non, mon ami, she's not here.*

Walking over to the bed, he grabbed his discarded pants and underwear. He really should take a shower but found himself unable to bear the thought of washing her scent away. Memories of last night flooded his mind—her sweet curvy body, her skin, her tight little pussy milking him—and he wanted to hurl something at the wall.

One night? Who was he kidding? It wouldn't be enough to slake his thirst for her. If anything, it only whetted his appetite. But damn, she already got what she wanted.

She was pregnant. With his pup.

The impact of it all hit him at once. When they were discussing it, it had been an abstract idea. A concept his mind couldn't wrap around. He only cared about getting into her pants. And now ...

He raked his fingers through his hair. This was why he had forgone sex for the last year. It complicated things and screwed with his mind. He had to stay focused on his goals.

Mika said he wouldn't be responsible for anything. A sperm donor, nothing more.

A bad taste formed in his mouth, and he held on to that thought. If he could just remember that that was all she wanted from him, it would be easy to forget last night. Yes, that was it. It was fucking, nothing more. He would do his time, get out, and be free of anyone's control. He should thank his fucking lucky stars.

————

Delacroix spent the rest of his Sunday back in HQ, hitting the gym in an attempt not to think about Mika or last night. He ran for over two hours on the treadmill, hit every machine twice, and knocked down two punching bags in the process. It was only when he felt the need to sleep that he trudged back to his room and collapsed into bed.

The next day, he went through the motions of his morning routine of physical conditioning, lunch, and then more training in the afternoon. But the entire time, all he could think of was heading up to the command room and seeing Mika. He thought of all the scenarios and what he would say to her, but each one seemed ridiculous. What excuse could he make to see her that wouldn't sound contrived? He got what he wanted, her body for the night, and there was no need to see her.

Despite all that, he found himself taking the elevator up to her floor anyway the first chance he got. Glancing over to her corner office, he saw the door was closed and the lights were out. *What the hell?* It was early afternoon, not even close to quitting time.

"Hey," he called to one of the pencil pushers walking by. "Where's the boss?"

The man shrugged. "She's not in today."

A cold feeling gripped his chest. "Is she okay? Did she call in? What did she say?" He grabbed him by the arm and shook him, as if that would make him answer faster. "Tell me now or—"

"I said, I dunno!" He pushed his glasses up his nose. "She just didn't show up, okay?" When Delacroix released him, he scampered away.

Mika didn't show up to work. Was that her way of avoiding him? A thought popped into his head, one that made his mood grow even darker. Perhaps she despised him and was ashamed of what they had done. She knew everything about him after all and maybe realized she had been slumming it by fucking lowly bayou trash like him.

He told himself he didn't care. He'd slept with fancy rich ladies before looking for a rough tumble before going back to their boring lives in the city. This shouldn't be any different. Then why was there a pain in his chest lodged so deeply he couldn't breathe?

The thoughts were consuming him, driving the need to see her again. But the next day, she didn't come back to work either. He stalked the garage looking for signs of her car, but it was nearly five o'clock, and she still hadn't show up. What was going on?

He marched to the elevator, hoping to take it to the command room to find some answers, but someone was already waiting inside.

"Delacroix, there you are." It was Wyatt Creed, dressed in one of his fancy suits, arms crossed over his chest.

"What do you want?"

He stared at Delacroix in his usual haughty manner. "Meeting in my office, now. Let's go."

"Can't it wait?"

"No."

Fuck this fils-putain. He had half a mind to tell him to pound sand, but Wyatt gave him an impatient "don't fuck with me" look that reminded him of Sebastian Creed. Though Wyatt wasn't a dragon like his father, Delacroix didn't underestimate him. The quiet ones were always the ones to watch out for.

When they reached central operations, Wyatt motioned to follow him to his office. When he stepped inside, he was surprised to find that it wasn't empty as two people were already waiting inside.

"Hello, Delacroix." Vrost's ice blue eyes pierced right into him. "Nice of you to finally join us."

"*Al Doilea,*" he said in a mocking voice as he used the Beta's traditional honorific.

"Actually, you should be calling me that." Astrid Jonasson-Vrost grinned at him. He remembered the young woman as she was also Queen Desiree's best friend. "I'm Beta now. Officially."

"Well, you're certainly a more welcome and lovely sight than your predecessor," he replied, then turned to Vrost. "Why didn't you invite me to your retirement party?"

Vrost snorted. "I just came here to give you the news personally. Just so you know it's official."

"What news?"

"You've been reassigned, Delacroix. From this point on,

you'll officially be part of the Lycan Security Force of New York, and you'll be guarding the Alpha."

Reassigned? But how—wait. Mika. Had he forgotten her end of the bargain? She promised him a cushy job and a chance to shorten his sentence.

"You don't look happy," Vrost remarked.

"I'm crying with tears of joy on the inside," he said sarcastically. "When do I begin?"

"As soon as possible," Astrid stated. "We can't let the mages get Lucas. If they capture him and get his blood, it could mean the end. With your powers, you could easily hide him in the shadows, right? And no one would find you guys?"

He nodded. "Yes, that's how it works. But doesn't the Alpha have adequate protection?"

Vrost's eyes glinted like hard flint. "From what we've learned, even if they had all three artifacts, the mages still need his or Adrianna's blood to activate whatever spell they're planning to use. We need to make sure that we have a way to take him out of the equation if that ever happens."

"Sounds like a brilliant plan." Delacroix could bet who came up with that one. Speaking of which ... "So, the boss lady's fine with that? Should I go and give her my farewell?"

"Mika?" The female's nose wrinkled. "Oh, you won't have time for that. Besides she's not going to be back anytime soon."

The information hit him like a ton of bricks slamming into his chest. "Not going to be back *soon*?"

"Yup." Her head bobbed up and down. "Things got too hairy in Russia, and she had to step in before we lost the alliance. Took the first plane out to Moscow this morning.

Don't know when she'll be back, but if I know Mika, she won't come back until the job's done."

"Yeah, definitely," he managed to croak out before the pain in his chest dug deeper. "She certainly finishes what she starts."

CHAPTER EIGHT

JFK International Airport was busier than usual. Perhaps the unseasonably warm winter weather was an incentive for tourists to flock to New York. The international arrivals was packed to the gills, and weary travelers trudged along the lines into the immigration booths.

"Welcome back to the United States, Ms. Westbrooke," the immigration officer said as he stamped the passport on his desk. "I'm sure after three months, you're happy to be back."

"I am," Mika answered automatically. "I can't wait to eat some bagels and cream cheese." *And maybe some pizza. And Chinese food.* God, she didn't know if it was the baby or being back in New York, but the moment the plane landed, all she could think about was food.

The officer slid her passport back to her and laughed. "Go on then. After a long flight, you're probably cranky and starving for a real meal. My wife was the same with each kid we had."

Realizing his gaze had briefly slid down to her growing belly, she quickly wrapped her coat around her. "Thank you, sir," she grumbled as she walked away. Didn't he know it was rude to remark on a woman's pregnancy unless her condition was explicitly stated?

Still it was a reminder for her to be careful. No one in the States knew about her pregnancy yet. In fact, the entire time in Russia, she had worked to conceal it too. It had worked for the first few weeks, but Natalia Ivanova had definitely remarked on it. The Russian Alpha had simply shrugged and said it was fairly obvious to anyone who'd been pregnant and that if she was trying to hide it, she had to do a better job. Rude, yes, but when you were Alpha of a clan of over a hundred Lycans, you could pretty much say anything you want.

An involuntary smile spread across her lips. Despite her tough-as-nails exterior, Natalia had a soft inside that she rarely showed to anyone. While most people thought of her as a bitch, Mika knew that she had no choice but to be one. Otherwise, no one would take her seriously or follow her orders, which would cause chaos within her clan. The negotiations with New York had been tough, if only to show her Lycans that she would not cower to any other clan. Meanwhile, Mika's presence in Moscow was a sign that New York was serious about the alliance. She had pleaded their case, telling them about the skirmishes and battles she'd personally fought in the war against the mages, which seemed to have earned the respect of the Russian Lycans and earned New York their much-needed alliance. In the next few weeks, they could start making plans to infiltrate the mage stronghold outside Moscow, which would be a big win for the Lycans.

Truth be told, she could have gone home after three

weeks, maybe even two. But it was Natalia who kept the negotiations going, strangely, after remarking on Mika's pregnancy. Had the other woman sensed her hesitation in going back to America? If that was the case, then she was grateful to her.

The last three months had allowed her to enjoy her pregnancy in peace, before the proverbial shit hit the fan. Her parents were already pissed that she missed Christmas and would be livid when they found out she kept her pregnancy a secret. They'd be happy about the baby but then they'd ask all kinds of questions. She was already dreading answering them.

Another reason she was glad for the distance was that with half a world between them, she wouldn't have to see Delacroix. Leaving that hotel room had been difficult, and she knew if she saw him again, that longing in her chest would never go away. She couldn't bear to be near him anymore, especially not when they acted like nothing happened between them. And certainly not when he eventually went back to his playboy ways and flirted with other females.

Surely by now, if she did see him again, her body wouldn't react the same way. It wouldn't ache for him as badly as it did the first few days, and she could act normal around him. And maybe her she-wolf too, wouldn't want to see him so badly. In the first few days, it had been a difficult to manage; if it wasn't moping around and sad, it was angry at her. Only when she reminded her animal that they had to take care of their pup now, and that was the most important thing in the world now, did it calm down. Her wolf became extra protective of her, and was distracted enough with keeping their pup safe that it didn't whine or rage at her for leaving Delacroix behind in New York.

Now that he was assigned to Lucas's security detail, there were less chances of seeing him. Hell, she could access his schedule anytime and make sure they never bumped into each other. Everything could stay exactly as they did now, with them living separate lives.

Though Lucas had offered to send a car to fetch her, she declined, saying it was easier to take a cab. She had asked him not to mention to her parents or siblings that she was flying back tonight, as one of them would insist on coming to get her. Dad or Nathan probably wouldn't notice, and Amanda or Knox would just shrug, but if her mother came, she would know something was up. And after flying for sixteen hours, she wasn't ready for that yet.

The cab stopped just outside the main entrance of The Enclave, and she accepted her suitcase from the driver with a warm thanks. She struggled to roll the suitcase along as she headed toward the glass doors. It was heavy because of all the damned souvenirs Natalia had insisted she take, and it fell over as it hit a crack in the pavement. "Fucking hell." As she bent down to pick up her suitcase, she stopped short when she felt the back of her neck prickle.

"Welcome back, *cher*."

She stood there, frozen to the spot. Slowly, she looked up to face him. Delacroix leaned by the building entrance; arms crossed over his chest. His hair had gotten slightly longer, and his beard was thicker too. He looked straight at her with those dark eyes. Ignoring the way her heart leapt into her throat at the sight of him and her wolf's frantic, longing howls, she managed to speak. "How did you know?" She had been so careful, even opting to fly commercial instead of having the Fenrir jet pick her up in case he somehow got wind of her arrival.

"That you were coming home tonight?" That lazy smile spread across his handsome face, but she didn't let it fool her into letting her guard down, not when she could clearly see the hardness in his eyes. "I was in the car when the Alpha picked up your call."

Damn it! Talk about bad luck. She should have sent an email. "All right, then. I'm tired, and I'm going home."

"I didn't figure you for a coward, Mika."

"Coward?" Her shoulders tensed up. "What the hell are you talking about?"

"Were you so afraid to face me that morning that you had to put half a world between us?" He stalked toward her with ground-eating steps.

"Excuse me?" she shot back. "Did you think I was going to back out on our deal? You did your part, and I made sure you got transferred, right? That's what you wanted."

"My *part*?" he said incredulously. "Our deal? You think that's what I was thinking of? What's been hauntin' me these last months? Why I'm here?"

"It's not?" Her heart pounded in her chest. "Then why the hell are you here, Delacroix?"

"You fool." He grabbed her arm. "I—"

A loud bang sounded right by her ear, followed by exploding concrete a split second later. *Gunshot.*

"What the—" Another shot rang out, and she howled as pain shot right in the center of her back. "Fuck!" She glanced down at her chest. The bullet must have gone through, because she could feel the wound sealing quickly, her flesh burning as it knit together—invulnerability was a side effect of her True Mate pregnancy.

"Mika?"

She looked at Delacroix's pale face and then glanced down. Blood began to spread across his chest, blooming like a poppy flower on his white shirt. "No!" she cried. Panic set in, but she pushed it down. Whoever shot at them was still out there, and she had to get them to safety. Slinging Delacroix over her shoulder, she darted toward the doors leading into The Enclave. Thank goodness for Lycan strength.

"Call the medical wing, now!" she screamed at the security guard manning the desk as she laid him on the floor. When his gaze landed on Delacroix, he turned pale but grabbed the phone and began to frantically dial.

The scent of blood filled her nostrils, making her want to vomit. "Goddammit, Marc!" she wailed. "Don't you fucking die on me."

"I don't understand. You—" He coughed then nodded at her chest.

She shrugged her coat off and poked at the hole the bullet made in her shirt to show him that wound had closed up. "Yes, I'm fine. Alive. I'll explain later. Just hang on, okay?" *Oh God, Oh God*. It was all coming back again. The accident. Joe. No, she couldn't do this again. "Please don't die. You can't die, you hear me? I swear I'm gonna kill you if you die."

He laughed, then winced in pain. "I'm sure you will. *Cher*, I need to tell—"

"Stand back."

Relief poured through her as she recognized Dr. Blake standing over her. He was dressed in his robe and slippers, his hair mussed, but eyes alert. She scooted away to give him space, but not too far that she couldn't keep her eyes on Delacroix.

"What happened?" Dr. Blake asked as he examined the wound.

"Gunshot." She took a deep breath. Everything would be okay now, but she had to stay calm. "Must have been a long-distance high-powered rifle. I didn't hear or see anyone else on the street. The bullet, it went through me, and then lodged in his chest."

The doctor blinked up at her in confusion, then she opened her coat to show him her belly. Having been the physician for most of the True Mate females, he understood quickly. "Looks like you were able to slow down the impact, and the wound's not deep. I just need to take the bullet out, and he'll be fine." Behind him, two nurses were wheeling in a gurney. "Let's take him to medical."

———

Mika couldn't—wouldn't—fall apart. *Not now.* Delacroix was going to be fine; he was a Lycan, unlike Joe. Dr. Blake would stitch him up, and he'd be walking around in a couple hours.

But someone tried to kill her and unknowingly, her baby and Delacroix. She had to find out who it was and then ... well, there was no saying what she would do them, other than it wouldn't be pretty.

The shooter probably used a high-powered sniper rifle from a distance, as she or Delacroix would have easily detected anyone coming for them at close range. Probably hid in the building across the street or in a car parked a few hundred yards away.

She rose up from where she was sitting on the couch. They would be long gone by now, but if she went out, she could search the area and—

The door to the medical wing waiting room flew open, startling her. "Mika! You're—*Jesus Christ!*" Lucas's expression turned from surprise to shock when his gaze dropped to the dark red stain across her sweater. "They didn't say you'd been hurt too." His arms wound around her. "Medical called me and—" He froze as soon as he pulled her to his body. Slowly, his arms lowered, and he stepped away. For the third time that night, the unflappable Alpha of New York looked flabbergasted. "Mika ... you're ..."

"Er, it's a long story." It was hot inside, so she'd taken off her coat. Wearing only her sweater and leggings, her baby bump would have been obvious, even if Lucas didn't feel it for himself.

The dark slashes of his brows drew together. "True Mate, huh? Well, where is he?" He glanced around, as if looking for someone. "Is he from the Moscow clan? Is he following you back?"

She mentally slapped her forehead. It hadn't even occurred to her anyone would think that. But then, it would be a good cover story, if she could just have some time alone to craft it. "Can we talk about it some other time? Someone tried to kill me." And hurt Delacroix.

Lucas sat them down on the couch. "Tell me everything."

She proceeded to tell him the events starting from when the cab dropped her off. Her voice faltered when she said Delacroix happened to be outside when she arrived—which was not a lie, technically—but Lucas didn't notice or remark if he thought she was keeping something from him.

"Do you think it could be the mages?" he asked.

"Who else could it be?"

"They've never targeted anyone individually, except for me and Adrianna. Why would they want to kill you?"

"That's what I need to find out. Maybe Daric or Cross will have some intelligence and—"

"*Michalina Jean Westbrooke. What in the world is going on?*"

Oh crap.

Alynna Westbrooke stood over her, hands on her hips, and Mika was reminded about all those times when she was a kid and had done something naughty.

Had she forgotten that her parents lived in The Enclave? And that Lucas or someone who had witnessed what happened would have immediately called Alynna Westbrooke to tell her that her daughter had been shot just outside the building?

Lucas looked at her sympathetically but could only shrug. "I'll, uh, go and wait for Astrid so I can brief her." Even the Alpha of New York knew not to get between a mother and her pup. He stood up and gave her hand a supporting squeeze.

"Hey, Mom," she greeted weakly.

A lot of people mistook Alynna for her older sister, as they were not only so similar-looking, but Alynna also didn't look her age. Though there were crow's feet in the corners of her emerald eyes and laugh lines around her mouth, her skin looked relatively smooth and youthful. Her hair was still dark as night, and with her petite stature, it was easy to mistake her for someone much younger.

"*Hey, Mom?* That's the first thing you have to say to me after three months?" Alynna's green eyes blazed with anger.

"What's up?" she offered, which only made Alynna's brows draw together furiously. "I'm fine, I promise."

"Why didn't you tell us you were coming back? I had to get a call in the middle of the night from Lucas that you were back, and there was a shooting and—" Her voice trembled, and Mika could see genuine concern in her eyes as tears pooled in the corner. "My baby. I thought you were—" Her face froze when her gaze lowered to Mika's chest. She sniffed the air, then let out a scream when she finally realized it was blood on her sweater. "What the hell? You said you were fine! Why isn't the doctor seeing to you!"

"Calm down, Mom!" Oh God, this was not how she wanted to start this conversation. "I'm fine, I—"

Alynna pulled her to her feet. "We're going in there and —what the fuck is that?" Her eyes went wide as she stared at the obvious bump on her stomach.

"I can explain."

"You better, young lady!"

"Mika! Are you okay, baby?"

Oh, Jesus. "Dad!"

Alex Westbrooke sprinted toward her and pulled her into a hug. "I came as soon as I heard. I was on overnight shift." When he let go of her his gaze went to her chest. "Fuck! What happened?"

"She's *pregnant*," Alynna stated.

He didn't seem to hear his wife as he continued to stare at the bloody stain on her sweater and his nostrils flared "Why are you covered in blood? You—" Her father's eyes nearly popped out their sockets as his gaze slowly dropped to her belly. "Oh. *Oh.*" Something must have short-circuited in his brain, because he just stood there with his mouth open.

"Explain," Alynna said, crossing her arms over her chest. "Now."

"H-how did this h-happen?" Alex stuttered.

Where to begin? "The usual way?" When both of them glared at her, she clamped her mouth shut.

"God, Mika!" Alynna began. "You disappear for three months—"

"I did not disappear, *Mother*. I was working in Russia, trying to negotiate an important alliance so we can win this war against the mages."

"You *leave* for three months, and then next thing we hear is that you're in a shooting and you come back pregnant? How did you even—" Her jaw dropped. "Wait, you're not hurt?"

She nodded.

"That means ... oh!" Her mother's face brightened; all traces of anger gone. "Oh, my God! You found him. Your True Mate."

Mika found herself buried in a flurry of arms and chests as her parents embraced her. "Mom, Dad, I can't breathe."

"Oh, sorry, baby," Alex stepped back. He cleared his throat. "Who is he? When are we meeting him?"

"Is he from Russia?" Alynna grabbed her hand excitedly. "He must be. How did you meet? Did you know right away?"

"Er, maybe we should—"

"Mika, are you all right?"

Oh, for God's sake. This was turning into a farce. Did they call the entire clan in here?

Astrid, the new Beta of the New York clan, strode into the waiting room, followed by Lucas and Nick Vrost.

"Astrid," she greeted. "And Nick. I'm surprised you're here."

"Zac had to stay with Annaliese," the former Beta said, referring to his granddaughter and Astrid and Zac's pup. "Welcome back."

"She found her True Mate," Alynna said. "Isn't that exciting?"

"Hello, someone also tried to kill me," she reminded them. "I think that's the more pressing matter."

"We'll get to the bottom of this," Lucas said.

"It has to be the mages," Astrid began. "But they've only gone after Adrianna or Lucas until now."

"That's what I said," Mika began. "We should—"

The door leading to the treatment rooms opened. Mika's heart skipped a beat, waiting for Dr. Blake to come out and relay Delacroix's condition, but to her surprise, the Cajun himself staggered out. His skin was still pale, and his chest was bandaged under his leather jacket, but he was upright.

"Mr. Delacroix." Dr. Blake followed behind him, an annoyed look on his face. "I told you, you can't leave yet. You need rest."

But he ignored the doctor and marched straight to Mika. "You're not hurt." When his gaze lowered to her belly, his eyes widened.

"Of course not," Alynna said. "She's carrying her True Mate's baby. It makes her invulnerable to almost anything."

Dread crept into her chest, and Mika prayed he wouldn't say anything. *We had a deal*, she said silently, trying to catch his eye. But he wouldn't meet her gaze as he continued to stare at her stomach.

"Oh no, are you moving to Russia?" Alynna cried. "I mean, I know you have to be with your True Mate, but Moscow is so far away."

"You met your True Mate while abroad?" Astrid inquired. "How cool."

"I didn't say—"

"Russia?" Delacroix snapped out of his trance. "What the fuck are they talking about?"

Anger emanated off him in waves, making her flinch. "I didn't say anything about my True Mate," she said and sent him a warning look that said, *and you better not either*.

But he wasn't listening to her as his obsidian eyes hardened. "How could she meet her True Mate in Russia when he's right here in New York?"

"Here?" Alynna looked at Alex and then back at her daughter. "I don't understand."

"Delacroix," she hissed. "Stop—"

"Me. *I'm* her True Mate. And that baby is mine."

The silence that filled the room made her ears ring. Five seconds later, chaos erupted.

"What does he mean—"

"Delacroix?"

"But you were in Moscow—"

"Did he—"

Mika held her hands up. "Stop, stop!" When the room quieted down, she turned to Delacroix. "We had a deal. We agreed not to tell anyone about ... this."

His mouth curled up into a sardonic smile. "*You* said you

weren't going to tell anyone I was the father. I don't recall agreeing to such a thing, *cher*."

"You and your stupid loopholes!" She wanted to scratch his eyes out.

"Did you know she was your True Mate?"

All eyes turned to Alex. His jaw was clenched and fists curled up at his sides.

"*Oui*. She figured it out. I didn't know anything about True Mates at that point."

The older Lycan's eyes narrowed. "But you didn't know she was pregnant."

"I ... did."

"You motherfucking bastard!" Alex lunged for Delacroix, but Lucas and Nick managed to restrain him. "You got her pregnant—"

"Oh, for God's sake, Dad." She put herself between Alex and Delacroix. "It takes two to tango. And should I remind you both that my birthday comes only seven months after your wedding anniversary?" Alynna turned bright red and Alex seemed to calm down. "My personal life is not up for discussion. Now if you'd all like to discuss who tried to end my *actual* life, then I'd be willing to talk."

"All right." Lucas stepped forward, raising his palms up. "It's late and we're all tired. There's nothing more we can do tonight. I think it's time we all went home." No one would disagree with the Alpha. Mika sent him a grateful smile.

The atmosphere in the room calmed down considerably. As her mother approached her, she shot her a warning look. "I'm not in the mood, Mom."

"Mika," she began as she gingerly placed an arm around

her shoulder. "I'm here, okay? The last couple of years have been hard with J—"

"I know." It wasn't that she didn't want to hear his name aloud. She still thought about Joe, but being away from New York, there were no memories of him around, nothing to remind her that he was dead and gone. Maybe it wasn't fair, but she had to try and move on. If not for her, then for her child. "We'll talk, I promise." Her father didn't say anything but hugged her fiercely. His scent and his strong arms nearly had her bawling, but she managed to get a grip.

Everyone slowly slipped out of the room; everyone except—

"I think we should talk, *cher*."

She whirled around to face him. "There's nothing to talk about." If he didn't nearly die, she would have wrung his neck for the chaos he caused.

His eyes flickered to her belly. "Isn't there?"

"This shouldn't come as a surprise," she pointed out. "You knew what you signed up for."

"I did."

"And so now, you need to stay out of my way."

A smile spread across his lips. "I changed my mind."

"You changed ..." *Jesus*, he was worse than a woman. "You can't change your mind again. I can't become *un*-pregnant."

"Oh no, *cher*." He stalked toward her, and for some reason, she felt like a rabbit being hunted by a predator. "I'm not talking about that. I'm talking about us."

"Us? What are you talking about?"

"You. And me." His fingers clenched together, as if he were trying to stop himself from reaching out to touch something. "All these months ... I know there's something there."

"Ha, you're delusional." She crossed her arms over her belly. "I haven't thought about you since I left." *Lie. Total lie,* a voice in her mind screamed. But she squashed that thought.

"You thought I was going to die tonight. And you were scared you were going to lose me. You cared."

Arrogant bastard. "I'm not a monster. I would have been scared for anyone."

"So you say."

She wished he would do ... something. Get angry. Shout at her. Or even try to touch her. It would give her a good excuse to kick his ass. But the way he remained still, those ebony eyes fixed on her as if he was thinking hard, was unnerving. The wheels in his head were turning as if he were making big plans. *Oh no.* Surely, he wasn't thinking that there could be anything between them. That wasn't the plan, damn it! "This doesn't change anything, Delacroix."

"So you say."

"And I'm having this baby by myself."

"So you say."

"You got what you want. You can't change the terms of our deal."

"So you—"

"I swear to God, I'm gonna claw your eyes out if you finish that sentence," she snarled.

The bastard grinned at her. "Come, *cher,* you should get some rest. Besides, it's bad for our baby—"

"*My* baby."

"So you—" He stopped when she shot daggers at him. "I'll escort you back to your place."

"You'll do no such thing." She held her hands up at him. "Stay away from me, Delacroix. Or else." She stormed out of the medical wing, indignant fury coursing through her veins. Her wolf yowled woefully, wanting to go back to Delacroix and see him. Scent him. The damned animal had gone from happy to excited to angry and now sad, that surely it was confused. She reminded it of their pup, but that only seemed to agitate the wolf.

What a fucking shitshow this night turned out to be. Maybe he'd been pumped with so much drugs that he had been hallucinating. Cared for him? He really was delusional. Well, surely the next few days couldn't get any worse. By morning, all those drugs would have been cleared out of his system, and he would leave her alone.

CHAPTER NINE

THREE MONTHS.

Delacroix didn't quite believe she would be gone that long. Truly, he didn't expect her to leave at all. He had gone through a maelstrom of emotions when she left. Anger. Betrayal. Disappointment. Yes, he knew they had a bargain, but he didn't plan on feeling this way. Wanting her so much, but not just her body. He wanted *her*. Wanted to be around her and know if she was sad or happy or angry. Wanted to see her every day and take a whiff of her wonderful scent. Wanted to see her body grow and change as she carried their child. His wolf felt exactly the same way, its mood swinging from melancholy to rage; miserable without her and furious at him for letting her get away.

But the days and weeks passed. He couldn't even get any news as to what was happening with her because he couldn't go to the GI headquarters since he was now officially part of the Alpha's security detail. Even Jacob couldn't tell him anything, and Lizzie was tight-lipped because Mika's mission was need-to-know only.

He tried to forget her, tried to distract himself with all kinds of activities, but nothing worked. When he tried to approach other women, he just felt disgust, especially when he came near another female and smelled her scent and realized they just weren't ... Mika.

After months of torture, he finally heard her name. Just his luck, he had been in the car with the Alpha when she called. His ears perked up, and he listened in, getting all the information he needed. Waited for her to come back to The Enclave. While he had appeared confident and relaxed, in truth, he'd been a nervous wreck. Seeing her again brought back all the memories. He couldn't even bring himself to be angry with her.

And then, all hell broke loose. God, he had been so scared when he saw the blood on her chest, he didn't even realize the bullet had gone into him. Why the hell didn't anyone tell him about pregnant True Mate females being invulnerable? Would have saved him a heap of trouble.

But, as scared as he had been last night, he was glad, because it proved one thing: Mika cared for him. As he lay there with the bullet lodged in his rib cage, he saw her face. Saw the concern and fear in her eyes and the words she said. *Please don't die. You can't die, you hear me?*

That was enough for him, to convince him that this whole thing of them being apart, with her raising their pup on her own, was wrong. She was his. The pup was his, and he was damned if he was just going to walk away from that.

But how was he going to get her to listen to him? He couldn't even get near her, not when she was all the way at the Brooklyn Bridge, and he was stuck guarding the Alpha. Even now, he desperately wanted to go to her, but he had the morning shift. He had escorted the Alpha from his penthouse in The Enclave and to his office.

And now, he was standing outside said office, waiting for the Alpha to leave for his lunch meetings. He wished he could just leave this cushy job and tell Vrost to stick it where the sun don't shine.

The door opened behind him, and he straightened his stance. He expected the Alpha to step out, but instead, it was the Beta.

"Delacroix," Astrid began. "Lucas wants to speak with you."

"With me?"

"Yes." She motioned for him to step inside. "I'll see you later."

His brows wrinkled. "You're not staying?"

"No, I have stuff to do."

Puzzled, he hesitated before going in. What could the Alpha possibly want with him? Not wanting to keep him waiting, he carefully crept inside. "Primul?" he asked, using the traditional honorific for one's Alpha. "You wanted to see me?"

As usual, Lucas Anderson sat behind his large desk. He was, perhaps, one of the few men Delacroix thought looked intimidating while wearing an expensive tailored suit as he signed documents. Power emanated from the Alpha, and even without a single word or movement, Delacroix's wolf cowered, recognizing the pure dominant nature of the other wolf. No doubt, Lucas Anderson was a trueborn Alpha.

"Sit down." Elegant fingers placed a gold fountain pen into its holder.

He did as he was told, choosing the seat just opposite from his desk. "What can I do for you, Alpha?"

"Let's not mince words, Delacroix." Eerie mismatched eyes stared into him, as if boring right into his soul. "I know everything about you. Where you came from. What you did before you came here."

He gritted his teeth but didn't flinch. "I'm not proud of what I did back then. If Vrost has told you about my past, then it's probably all true." While Nick Vrost was a bastard, he wasn't a liar.

"So, you don't deny it? All the stuff you did? No excuses?"

"No." He could make excuses. Blame it all on Remy. On being scared to disobey his orders. But he knew there was always a choice. "You know what Pont Saint-Louis's reputation is. How we make our living. You could have turned me away."

Lucas nodded. "I know. But I was intrigued by what Nick said you could do."

He didn't want to think of that night. Wanted it erased from his memories. "I thought we weren't mincing words, Alpha. So, did you call me in here to kick me out?" Going Lone Wolf now wouldn't be so bad. He had some money tucked away from the last year. He could even give King Karim a call, and he would offer him a place back at the palace in a heartbeat. But that would mean leaving New York, and he couldn't do that. Not now.

The Alpha threaded his fingers together and leaned forward on his desk. "What are your intentions toward Mika?"

"And this is your concern because ..."

"Because I'm her Alpha. And her family."

He didn't conveniently forget that fact. Everyone knew she was the Alpha's cousin. "That pup is mine. I intend to be a father to the child."

"And Mika?"

"I intend to have her too. If she would have me." *And she will.* She had to.

For a moment, he thought the Alpha would lunge at him, the way her father did last night. To his surprise, he grinned instead. "Good." His shoulders relaxed. "Mika's a tough nut to crack, so you'll have a challenge ahead of you."

He blinked, wondering if he'd heard right. "I ... I don't understand." The Alpha was giving him his blessing to go after his cousin? Even after knowing about his past?

"You're True Mates," he stated. "You're meant to be together. The sooner you both accept it, the happier you both will be. God knows, if anyone deserves to be happy, it's Mika."

From his tone, there was a lot of meaning behind those words, but for now, he couldn't quite unpack everything that was happening. But he knew not to look a gift horse in the mouth. "Thank you, Alpha. I don't know what to say."

"Just say you'll win her over." He rose up from his chair. "I don't know how you did it, being away from her all these months. It would have driven me crazy." His gaze flickered to the frame on his desk, the one Delacroix knew contained a photo of the Lupa and his son. "I can't even stand to be away from them during the day. Now," the Alpha patted him on the shoulder. "Let me give you a little push in the right direction."

As the Alpha told him what he had planned, Delacroix

couldn't help but grin as hope bloomed in his chest. *You better watch out, cher.* He was coming for her, and coming fast and hard. Mika wasn't going to know what hit her before it was too late.

CHAPTER TEN

"WELL, IT'S NOT LIKE THERE'S ANY USE HIDING IT NOW," Mika grumbled to herself as she strode into HQ. She had thought of bundling up in loose sweaters and jackets, but as she got dressed this morning, she said, *fuck it*, and put on a tight sweater dress and leggings.

As soon as she got to the command floor, a hush came over the room. Several people quickly scrambled to their desks, and one of the junior analysts accidentally ran into one of the glass partitions as he stared at her belly when he walked by.

"Something the matter, Ryerson?" she barked.

"N-n-no, ma'am!" The young man rubbed the growing knot on his forehead as he scampered away.

Head held high, she headed straight to her office. She'd had a long day yesterday—and an even longer night—and now today wasn't going to be short either. Work had piled up in her absence, and she was going to have to put in extra time. Not to mention, it was obvious no one was going to get any work done, not when everyone would be talking about *how the boss came back from Russia knocked up.* Hopefully, all of this would die down in a few days, and they could all get back to the important work of, oh, what was that again? *Oh yeah,* saving their very existence.

Focusing on work had always been the way she coped, and so the morning went by quickly as she plowed through the pile of emails, paperwork, and calls. Her stomach growled by mid-morning despite the huge breakfast she'd had. But that was the consequence of having a True Mate baby. She was starving all the freakin' time.

Thankfully, she still had two ham and cheese bagel sandwiches in her purse. She unwrapped those and made quick work of them, then washed it all down with a swig of coffee right before her conference call with the Toronto Alpha. By noon, she was starving again. Hmmm, maybe a pepperoni pizza would be good for lunch.

"Really?" She stared down at her belly. "We haven't even been in America for twenty-four hours. Don't you miss caviar and borscht?"

"Hey, sweetie!" came a cheerful voice as the door to her office opened. Alynna walked in, two large paper bags with "Emerald Dragon" stamped on the side. "I brought lunch."

She looked up and raised a brow. "You could knock."

"I'm your mother." As she placed the bags on the table, the smell of orange chicken, fried rice, and egg rolls wafted into her nostrils, and her stomach growled audibly. "See? I came just in time."

"For my noon feeding," she said with a sigh.

"Aww, baby." Alynna walked over to her side and squeezed her shoulder. "I know what it feels like. You're starving all the time. Your body is changing. Feet swelling.

Nausea. Don't worry, if you have any questions, I'll be happy to answer them. This is my first grandchild after all."

Though she wanted to be mad at her mother for just barging in here, Mika really couldn't. After all, she had kept her pregnancy a secret from her. When she and Joe had been trying for a baby, she always knew her mother would have been the first person she would have given the news to. "I ... thanks, Mom." Before she could say anything else, a knock interrupted her. "Come in."

The door swung open, and Mika readied herself for some emergency or another fire she had to put out. But she was not prepared to see Delacroix casually walking into her office. "What are you doing here?" She shot up to her feet. "You're not allowed in here." Her wolf, on the other hand, seemed to disagree, as the little bitch practically rolled over and showed her belly when he walked in. And it didn't help that he looked incredibly handsome and sexy with his hair slicked back, wearing a dark, well-fitting suit, the usual uniform for the Alpha's bodyguards. Did nothing look terrible on the man?

He flashed her that devastating smile. "Of course I am, *cher*. I'm allowed wherever you are."

She marched over to him, ignoring the way her stomach fluttered with happiness at the sight of him. *You're just happy he's not dead*, she told herself. *Now you can kill him.* "I don't know who the hell you think you are, walking in here like this, but you better leave in the next second or I'll have someone throw you out into the East River."

"I know exactly who I am, *cher*. I'm your new bodyguard," he said cheerfully.

"Body ... guard? You're joking, right?"

"*Non*, I wouldn't joke about such a thing. The Alpha himself assigned me to guard his cousin after the attempt on her life by our enemies. I'm supposed to stay close and make sure no danger comes to you."

Her jaw dropped all the way to the floor. "No."

"*Oui*."

"Lucas ..." Her hands clenched tight. "And he didn't even come here himself to tell me." *Coward*. "You can bet he and I are going to have a little talk about this."

"Whatever you want, *cher*." He turned to Alynna. "I don't believe we've been introduced." His tone was dripping with charm. "I'm Marc Delacroix, at your service. And you must be Mika's older sister."

"Ohhh, a charmer." Alynna's tone was filled with mirth. "I think I like you."

Oh brother, just what she needed. Him and her mother getting along.

"Apologies if I interrupted your lunch, ladies."

"I'm suddenly not hungry," she groused. "You both can leave now. I have a lot of work."

"Oh, this is good," Alynna said with a chuckle.

She glared at her mother. "You find this funny?"

"I find it *ironic*." She glanced at Delacroix. "Her father was *my* bodyguard too."

"Then I hope she inherited both your beauty *and* intelligence."

"Argh!" She was so mad she was shaking. "If you think—"

Alynna cleared her throat. "You know what? I have this appointment I have to get to. Enjoy the food." After a quick kiss to her cheek, she dashed out the door.

Goddammit, was everyone conspiring against her? "What are you doing?"

Delacroix had reached into the paper bags and was opening the contents. "Tsk, tsk, this food isn't good for you, *cher*. Too much artificial flavoring. Oil. MSG." He glanced at the empty coffee cup on her table. "Caffeine? You shouldn't even be having that."

"*Excuse me*?" She snatched away the container in his hand.

"You should be having healthy food, with lots of calcium and folic acid—"

"Look, I don't know who you think you are, but you can't barge in here and start judging me on my food choices."

"I'm your bodyguard, I need to look out for your well-being." He plucked the box of fried rice out of her hand.

"You're supposed to watch out for flying bullets or car bombs." She took it back and placed it on the desk behind her. "Now, I don't know what you and Lucas have cooked up, but this isn't going to work."

"If you say so."

God, he was infuriating. "What do you want, Delacroix? Are you hoping Lucas would free you from your servitude if you played concerned dad-to-be?" A terrible feeling crept into her chest. "Is that it? Trying to sweet talk me and so then Lucas will—" She gasped when he suddenly lunged forward and trapped her between her desk and his body.

"This has nothing to do with the Alpha. Or anyone else except you and me." Fury flared in his eyes, but then subsided just as quickly. "You know what I want."

"No, I really don't."

"I told you that night. I want *you*."

Fucking hell, those words sent a ripple of desire straight to her core. "For that night," she huffed.

"No, not just for that night."

She ignored the way her heart beat like a drum against her rib cage. "Well, I don't want you."

"Really?" He bent his head down closer, his breath skimming against her ear. "You wanted me just fine then. Or have you forgotten it already? I could remind you."

"Damn you!" She pushed him away. "*That* will never happen again. Get out!"

His eyes stared at her defiantly, then lowered to her lips and down to the rest of body like a lazy caress. The heat from his gaze seemed enough to make her nipples tighten, and she bit her lip to keep from moaning out. All he had to do was touch her, and she would be a goner. "I'll be outside. Just say the word if you need me."

She couldn't help but track him as he left, and when the door closed behind him, she let out an outraged scream. "Son of a bitch!" She fell back, bracing herself on the desk as her knees turned to jelly. *Deep breaths. Deep breaths.* But that only made it worse. His scent still lingered in the air, and her wolf just loved it, the tramp.

"Damn it!" Why was she feeling this way? She thought she'd gotten past wanting him. The ache that had been so keen when she first left had dulled in the cold Russian winter. In fact, she thought she'd all but conquered it. But all he had to do was come near her, and her body was all but panting for him, bringing back memories from that night.

Hormones, she told herself. Her mom had said her body was changing. Maybe she was getting to that time when her body was craving sex. Plus, it had been too long. Not like she had any chances of getting some in Russia. *Yeah, that was it.*

With a deep sigh, she walked back around to her chair and began unpacking the food. Lunch first, then a phone call to Lucas. Her cousin was going to have a lot of explaining to do, after she ripped him a new one.

———

It took about twenty phone calls, but she managed to get a hold of Lucas, but only by calling Sofia's phone and asking to speak to him. Much to his credit, he let her rant and rave, but told her that he was not changing his mind, then hung up.

She fumed for the rest of the day and didn't leave her office at all for the rest of the afternoon. It wasn't difficult, but with Delacroix standing outside her door like some sentinel, there wasn't much incentive for her to leave. Frankly, if she hadn't run out of food, she would have been happy to stay inside here forever. She could order in, but that would mean having to open the door. If only Daric or Cross were around, but they were busy, and she doubted getting her a pizza was a top priority right now.

So, after turning off her computer and shutting off the lights, she yanked her office door open. "I'm done for the day," she said before Delacroix could say anything.

He gave her one of those devilishly handsome smiles. "Let's go then. I was getting hungry, and I'm sure you are too. We can have dinner on the way back to The Enclave."

She froze. "Excuse me?"

"Dinner. You know, the meal in the evening?"

"I know what dinner is." Unfortunately, her stomach decided it was the perfect time to growl loudly.

"Sounds like you're ready," he said with a grin. "Come."

"I'm not having dinner with you."

"Then I'll stand next to you," he said. "But you will be having a healthy meal, not that trash you ate today."

"A bullet ripped right through me. I think a little caffeine and MSG won't hurt me," she pointed out. "I've been fine the last couple of months, eating what I want. And you won't be coming with me anywhere."

"Then how are you leaving then?"

She scrunched up her nose. "I'll be driving myself."

He dangled something in front of her. "Might be difficult without these."

"What—my keys." She tried to grab it from him, but he raised it high so she couldn't reach it. "How did you—did you steal them from my desk? Give them back." When her attempts to take the keys back failed, she crossed her arms over her chest and pouted.

"Are you hungry or not? Come, *cher*." His hand touched her elbow gently, which still sent a frisson of electricity up her arm. "Before the traffic gets too bad."

She allowed him to lead her to the garage and to her car but was grumbling most of the way. Breaking free of his grasp, she headed to the passenger-side seat.

He slid into the driver's side. "Seatbelts please."

"Yeah, yeah."

The engine roared to life, and soon they were driving out of HQ. As they left the secret entrance, he slowed as they reached the end of the alley, then stopped completely before pulling out to the street. He barely hit twenty as he drove them up Broadway.

"Can you possibly drive any slower, gramps?"

He didn't say anything, just kept his eyes on the road.

"Where are we stopping for dinner?" she asked with an irritated sigh when they passed Canal St.

"Don't you worry, we're nearly there."

As he took one of the many smaller streets off Broadway, she recognized the trendy SoHo neighborhood. "Wait, are you going to Muccino's?"

He answered by stopping right in front of the Italian restaurant. "I figured you missed the food here."

Oh. Dear. Her chest tightened. She didn't even realize how *much* she missed Muccino's until they were already here. So many good memories growing up. So many birthdays, anniversaries, celebrations. She cleared her throat, trying to dislodge the lump that was lodged there.

"Is this all right?" He reached over to brush her cheek with his knuckles.

"It's fine," she croaked, then unbuckled her seatbelt and reached for the door so she could step out. The winter air cooled down the blush in her cheeks, and she quickly strode toward the restaurant's door, not even waiting for him. He could park the damn car himself since he stole her keys.

"Welcome to Muccino's, do you have—Mika?"

She stopped short at the familiar voice. Well, the voice was familiar, but she wasn't sure if she was imagining things. "Isabelle?" She *must* be imagining things because she couldn't believe the young woman in front of her was Isabelle Anderson.

Her cousin grinned at her from behind the hostess

station, mismatched blue and green eyes sparkling. She strode over and enveloped her in a tight hug. "Oh my God, Mika. Mama told me you were back home! And—" She stepped back and looked at her belly. "Congrats! I wouldn't have believed it until I saw it."

"I—thanks." She was still flabbergasted as she stared at the young woman; where was the flighty young fashionista they all knew? Usually, Isabelle was decked from head to toe in designer brands. Now, she was wearing a plain white blouse, black pencil skirt and sensible shoes. Her face had only the barest of makeup, and her hair was pulled back into a sleek ponytail. "H-how are you? When did you start working here?"

"A couple of weeks ago," she said. "The manager and the hostess quit at the same time, which meant Mama had to take over." Muccino's was run and owned by Frankie Anderson's family, the former Lupa of New York and Lucas's mother. "So ... I thought I'd help out too." She seemed almost shy and demure, not at all like the bubbly young woman Mika remembered. But then again, her whole life had changed a year ago.

"How's Evan?" she asked, referring to Isabelle's young son. "He must be what ... seven months now?"

"Almost eight, and he's great." Genuine happiness and love lit up her face. "Papa's watching him at home. He's loving being a grandpa, and sometimes he and Mama'll have all four kids at the same time. It's chaos, but they're so thrilled by them all. And—oh, hey, D!"

Her spine tensed as she felt a hand splay over the small of her back. Her attempts to shrug him away only brought mild amusement to his face. "Isabelle," he greeted. "How have you been? Is the job treating you well? How's the little one?"

Mika's gaze bounced from her cousin to Delacroix. "You know each other?"

"Yeah, he's always around Lucas, being his bodyguard and all," Isabelle said. "I'm great, D, and so's Evan. You should see all the new tricks he's learning."

"I'd like to see that," he said, flashing her a friendly smile.

An uncomfortable feeling crept into Mika's middle as she watched the friendly, familiar banter between the two. "Can I get a table, Isabelle?" It took all her might not to snap at her cousin. "I'm hungry."

"Oh, of course." She grabbed two menus and led them into the main dining room, toward a cozy dim booth in the corner. "Your server will be right with you. Gio's not working tonight," she said, referring to their cousin, Uncle Dante's son. "Otherwise I'd have seated you at the chef's table in the back."

"Thank you," she said curtly. She couldn't help it, not when the only thing she could focus on was Isabelle and Delacroix's familiar banter. Did they also see each other outside of the restaurant? Just the thought made a hot, tight ball form in her chest.

Delacroix raised a brow at her but made no comment. "Thank you, Isabelle."

Mika slid into the booth and picked up a menu, raising it up to block her face. She didn't really need to read the menu because she'd practically memorized the entire thing, but she just didn't want to keep on watching the two of them flirting.

"I'll have your waiter come by to take your drink orders."

She nodded dismissively at Isabelle, and the younger

woman strode back toward her station. Delacroix moved into the booth, staying near the other end, and picking up the menu. When he didn't say anything, she said, "I didn't realize you two were close." The words came out of her mouth unexpectedly.

Slowly, he put his menu down. "The Alpha and Lupa visit her a lot, since she lives in the same building as them. She's a lovely young woman. And her son's adorable too. The first week she was here, she couldn't find a babysitter, so she brought him along. I was here with the Alpha and he offered to watch Evan for an hour. Is there something wrong with that?" He stared at her with those dark eyes filled with amusement.

"I didn't say there was. But you should know, Isabelle's been through a lot. I don't want her getting hurt."

"Of course you don't. No one does. Her family is protective of her as they should be, but she's much tougher than she seems."

"Is that so?" That hot sensation in her chest coiled tighter. "You know her that well?"

"She had a baby all alone while being not much of an adult herself. You shouldn't underestimate her."

So, he knew all about Isabelle's situation. What other secrets did they confide in each other? "Just be ... be careful."

Confusion passed over his face as his dark brows drew together. "Careful of ..." Then his eyes lit up, and his lips turned at the corner. "Are you jealous?"

"No!" She slammed the menu down so hard it made a thwacking sound on top of the table. "What the hell are you talking about? I'm not jealous of anyone."

The irritating smile he wore on his face made her want to

smack him with something. "Sure. Of course not." Turning his attention back to his menu, he began to thumb through it.

She let out a huff, staring at him, waiting for him to argue. But the infuriating man ignored her. Thankfully, their waiter came to take their orders.

The rest of their dinner went by in relative peace and silence. He didn't seem to object to the meals she ordered— ravioli, veal scaloppine, and a steak—but he did keep trying to push the extra veggie sides at her, which she promptly shot down with a freezing stare. When the server came back asking if they wanted coffee or tea after dessert, Delacroix dismissed him before she could order, which made her glare harder at him. When the young man came back and dropped a black folder at their table, he reached for it, but she immediately snatched it away.

"Don't you dare," she fumed. She dropped a couple of bills into the folder and pushed it toward him. "That's my half. I don't need any change."

Not bothering to wait for him, she got up and made a beeline toward the exit. Then she realized he still had the car keys, and she also had no idea where he'd parked. "Damn it!'

"Did you have a nice dinner?" Isabelle asked as she came up to her.

"Of course, delicious as always, though you know I can always tell when it's not Uncle Dante or Gio cooking."

She laughed. "I'll be sure to mention it to them. So ..." She glanced back toward the dining room. "You and Delacroix, huh?" Her eyes dropped down to her belly.

"You know?" she asked incredulously. "Of course you know." A long sigh escaped her lips. "Everyone knows, right?"

"Yeah, Lucas told us. Even Julianna knows, and she's all the way in Zhobghadi. Hey"—she put a hand on Mika's shoulder—"I'm happy for you, I really am. He's a great guy."

"Oh yeah, well, maybe you should have him. You two seem cozy." Too late. A look of grief crossed Isabelle's pretty face. "Jesus, I'm sorry. I'm an asshole, Isabelle." She should have been more sensitive to her cousin, after what had happened. No one knew the exact story, really, only that she'd met her True Mate and had gotten pregnant, but he wasn't in her life anymore. She wouldn't tell anyone who he was or if he was even alive. No, Isabelle didn't deserve any of the vitriol Mika had spewed, and she should have known better. "Forgive me, Isabelle. I don't have an excuse speaking to you that way, other than that I'm a raging bitch."

She smiled at her weakly. "No, it's fine. Really. But D ... he doesn't ... I mean ... he gets all flirty and all, but that's all he does. I even heard that ... well, I've been talking to Julianna, who's been talking to Deedee. She wanted to get the skinny on Delacroix, and according to Dee, he'd been on his best behavior the entire time he was there. Never went on a date or got together with any of the girls at the palace."

What? Surely that wasn't true. But before she could ask Isabelle any more about what she knew about Delacroix, the man himself came up to them. "Shall we head out, *cher*?"

She nodded, not knowing what to say. After saying goodbye to Isabelle, he led her outside toward where he parked the car across the street. Her mind was still in shock from what Isabelle had revealed that she let him open the door for her, and she went in automatically.

The drive back to The Enclave was silent and took no time, thankfully. When he pulled into her parking space, she let him open the door for her once again. "You can go home now," she said. "I doubt I'll get attacked between here and my apartment."

"I *am* home," he said matter-of-factly.

"What?"

"I live here too. In Center Cluster, actually, next to the Alpha's building."

Of course he did. "Fancy. Good for you." She turned and walked away, ignoring his chuckle. *Stupid ass.* He might think he was so smart, somehow charming Lucas into making him her bodyguard. But if he thought she was just going to let him walk all over her and bully his way into her life, well, he had another think coming.

CHAPTER ELEVEN

"Hello, neighbor," Delacroix greeted as soon as she opened the door of her apartment the next day.

"You again," she groused. Having had no time to go grocery shopping, she didn't have any food or coffee at home, and she was starving. "What are you doing here? And how did you know where I live?"

He held up a large paper bag. "I have breakfast. Why don't you let me in and—"

She snatched the bag from his hand. "I don't have time today. I'll eat in the car."

He didn't return her car keys last night, so she let him drive, too tired, hungry, cranky, and jet-lagged to argue. They were pulling out of the garage when she opened the paper bag. "What the heck is this?"

"Food, *cher*," he said.

She opened the top off one container and stared at the gray goop inside. "Oatmeal? You said you got breakfast."

"*Oui*. That's a healthy breakfast. There's also fruits, yogurt, a vegetable omelet, and some toast."

"Where's my coffee?"

"Coffee?" he scoffed. "I have orange juice and milk in the back seat, so you can have some folic acid and calcium."

If she wasn't so hungry, she would have screamed at him. "I was going to get pancakes, scrambled eggs, and bacon."

"Then good thing I came along, eh?"

God, she wanted to wipe that smug grin off his face. Instead, she reached into the bag and pulled out a spoon, shoveling as much oatmeal as she could into her mouth in as short an amount of time as she could so she didn't have to taste it. It abated the gnawing hunger in her stomach at least. As she was about to dig through the bag for more of the food, she stopped and glanced over at Delacroix.

Today he wasn't wearing his suit, but instead donned his usual attire of T-shirt and jeans, his leather jacket slung in the back of his seat. He didn't bother to ask her if she wanted him in uniform as her—she snorted—bodyguard, but that was him in a nutshell. Never asked, only did what he wanted, like worming his way into this position.

As he maneuvered the car with a relaxed ease, she couldn't help but stare at his muscled forearms, the way the veins under the tattooed skin twitched as he changed the gear or turned the wheel. His scent wafted over to her nostrils, which her hussy of a wolf just *loved*. His handsome face was scrunched up in concentration—why had she never noticed that little line between his brows, and why did she want to just reach over and touch it?

He suddenly looked over to her and realizing she was staring, flashed her a grin. "See something you like, *cher*?"

"No." She grabbed a piece of toast, shoved it in her mouth, and stared out at the road ahead. *Stop it*, she told herself. No staring. No looking. And definitely no touching.

For the next two weeks, she had to endure his hovering over her. He was the first person she saw in the morning and the last before she went home. He always brought her her meals or took her to dinner, and she was just too busy so she let him. While she grumbled about his food choices, he seemed to learn which foods she liked and which she didn't, and as long as she always ate the healthy stuff, like broccoli and kale, he made sure that she got something she actually wanted for the next meal, like pizza or tacos. Also, he glared and terrorized anyone who came near her, especially Dan, who, after a couple of days, just suddenly gave up even trying to talk to her. But, if anyone at GI had any opinions about his position as her bodyguard, they didn't say anything, not even Wyatt or Lizzie whenever they had their morning meetings and he hung around the command floor.

"Any news on our shooter?" she asked Lizzie.

She shook her head, her pigtails swishing over her shoulders. "Sorry, Mika. I've exhausted most of my contacts. The mages must have used a professional that's not from their usual list of contractors. I'll talk to Astrid again, see if our guys got any more evidence."

On the evening of the shooting, Astrid, Nick and the other members of the Lycan Security Force had searched the entire street. They found a car that had been abandoned a couple of hundred yards away. It had been modified so the shooter could lie down inside the trunk as he pointed his rifle through a hole drilled in the side of the vehicle. The shooter was definitely human as he left no trace scent except his sweat and urine, which told them he had been waiting there a long time. The gun was nowhere to be found, but they deduced he either took it with him or dumped it in the Hudson River.

"Thanks, Lizzie," she said. "If you guys are good, we're done here."

As they left the conference room, she saw Delacroix chatting with Jacob just outside the door. "Hey, Mika," Jacob greeted. "Welcome back. Sorry I haven't been by to say hi. Cliff's been keeping us busy with torture—er, training."

"Nice to see you too, Jacob." An idea struck her. "Say, it's been a while since Delacroix's done any training." She smirked at him. "Wouldn't want him to lose his touch."

"Lose my touch?" he asked indignantly.

"Why don't you take him to training for the afternoon?" she suggested. "In fact, it's an order. I'll be sure to tell Cliff what's happening, that he needs to make sure you're in your best shape since the guy who tried to shoot me is still out there."

And so, for the rest of the day, she was finally free of him. No more hovering outside her office, intimidating any of the analysts who came near her. Sure, she missed his presence during lunch when no one was around to bring her food. And if she kept finding herself looking out onto the command floor every now and then, she told herself it was just because she wanted to make sure no one was slacking off, and not because she was waiting for him to stroll in. When it was close to quitting time and he still wasn't back, well ... he had the car keys, so she had no choice but to go down to the training rooms to find him.

The GI's combat floors consisted of a main training hall with all the state-of-the art gym equipment, a sparring area, and a running track that ran around the room. It was modeled after the fifteenth floor of the Lycan Security Force's training room, including the dormitories, common rooms, and kitchens on the floor below for their agents. Mika herself had lived there for a year when she was a trainee. She walked over to the main sparring area, and it looked like they had just dismissed them for the day. Jacob was there chatting with Cliff, but where was Delacroix?

Her question was answered by a girlish, high-pitched giggle, which made her ears hurt. Turning toward the source, she saw the pretty young blonde by the leg press machine, a wide grin on her face as she looked up at the man beside her. "Oh, Marc, you're *so* funny." Her hand brushed his bicep.

A burning rage shot through her, and her inner wolf growled at the female who dared touch what was theirs.

Theirs?

"Mika?"

Holy hell, when did she walk toward them? Straightening her shoulders, she mustered the coldest tone she could. "If you're done here, I'd like to go home."

Delacroix's gaze darted from her to the blonde, an amused look on his face. "I have to go, Shelly."

"It's *Shelby*." The blonde's face twisted in anger for a fleeting second, before her sweet as sugar expression returned. "I'll see you around, Marc."

He gave her a curt nod before turning to Mika. "Shall we head out now, Ms. Westbrooke?"

The way he addressed her so formally shouldn't have annoyed her, but it did. "Fine."

"Where would you like to have dinner tonight?" he asked

as they reached her car. As always, he opened the door for her, and she slipped inside.

"Nowhere."

"You can't—"

"I have food at home," she said. "Just take me home, all right?" She didn't want to argue, not tonight.

"As you wish."

Not wanting to make further conversation, she turned the radio on, the music blaring out the speakers. He seemed to take a hint and didn't attempt any conversation. When they arrived, she dashed out of the car.

"Mika, wait!"

She walked fast, but he was much faster than her. When he got in front of her, she stopped before she collided into him. "Fuck," she muttered. "Goddammit."

"What's the matter, *cher*?"

"What's the matter?" she repeated. "*What's the matter? Let me tell you what's the matter:* My feet hurt, and I feel fat, and none of my clothes or shoes fit. I'm so hungry all the goddamn time that a third of my day is wasted just eating, but then I wake up feeling nauseous. I have to pee every five minutes, which is really annoying when I have to be on conference calls with boring Alphas that go on for days. Some days I just want to chug down an entire bottle of wine, but I can't stand the smell of alcohol. My breasts feel like water balloons being pumped bigger every day, and my nipples are starting to look weird. Not to mention, I'm so fucking horny, bumping up next to a dryer might set me off!" She let out a squeak and covered her mouth. *Dear God*, she prayed, *I promise if you sent a lightning bolt to kill me now, you can reincarnate me as anything you want. A snail. Or a badger.*

"Cher—"

"Please." She covered her face with her hands. "I'm so embarrassed."

"Mika." He gently pulled her hands away from her face. "You don't have to be embarrassed. Not with me."

"I'm sorry I went off on you like that."

"You're pregnant, you're allowed to be moody. Your body is changing, and that's normal."

"You sound like one of those pregnancy books. Maybe I should have read more up on this. I just ... feel so unprepared." She'd wanted this child for so long, that she didn't even think about what needed to be done before it actually arrived. "I haven't even seen Dr. Blake for an appointment."

"I don't think anyone can fully prepare for something like this, *cher*," he said. "But you should let me help you."

"You can't help me," she said.

"I can ... especially with that last one."

"I—that last one?"

"You know, about being horny—ouch!"

"Fuck off, Delacroix," she said, swatting him on the arm.

He laughed like a hyena. "I only meant that I know a good laundromat around the corner. What did *you* think I meant?"

"Laundromat—oh you!" She smacked him again, but it only made him chuckle harder. Unable to stop herself, she began laughing too.

"See, *cher*? There's no need to be worried. Everythin' will be all right," he drawled.

"I ... you're right. Thank you." With a final nod at him, she turned around and headed into the elevator lobby. Dear Lord, what happened back there? These damned hormones, making her go crazy. Telling him all about her swollen feet, her bathroom problems, and ... oh that last one. Being so horny all the time. It was true though, she was. But for some reason, that didn't really start until she got back and was around him all the time. Maybe she should just ask him—

No, that was a stupid idea. It was the most idiotic idea in the world right now, even if her hormone-fueled body thought otherwise. She would have to forget about it and never mention or think about it again.

———

The problem with saying you should never think about something ever again was that it only had the opposite effect. She thought about it. Again and again. And the more she did, the more her brain began to rationalize the merits of such an idea.

Orgasms releases oxytocin into your brain, which is good for you, and what's good for you is good for the baby.

Studies have shown that sex during pregnancy lowers blood pressure.

You've already done it before, what's the big deal?

Oh yeah, remember that thing he did in the bathroom with his mouth? And what about when he pushed you up against the—

"Argh!"

"Mika, you all right?" Cliff asked, his head cocked to the side.

She blinked. Did she just drift off in the middle of talking with Cliff? "Uh, yeah." *Damn it, brain, why do you do this to me?* "Can you repeat that last part again?"

If Delacroix had any idea she was having such a crisis, he didn't show it. After yesterday, he acted as he usually did. Even more helpful, if that was possible. Which was why she felt terrible asking him to go out on several errands outside because she didn't want to be around him. Her damn horny body was conspiring with her brain, and she feared she would jump him. Why did he have to be so hot? And handsome? And so nice to her that it made her want to cry.

Hormones, remember?

Of course, now that she was done for the day, she once again had no way of getting home, because Delacroix seemed to have taken ownership of her car keys. She made a mental note of getting her spare keys from her brother and closed up her office. Delacroix had to be around somewhere. She decided to head to the training floor in case he was hanging out with Jacob. She took the elevator down, drumming her fingers lightly on her arm as she waited for the car to reach her destination. When the doors opened, the sight that greeted her nearly made her wolf burst to the surface.

"You're such a sweetheart, Marc." Shelly or Shelby or whatever her name was, had a hand wrapped around Delacroix's forearm. "I'm looking forward to that lesson, then."

He pulled his arm away. "I told you, only if—Mika?" Their gazes met, and his dark eyes widened in astonishment. "Mika, this isn't—"

Her finger jabbed at the close door button, and he was probably too shocked to even try and stop it. *Or he was too occupied with that blonde bimbo.* An ugly, hot feeling coiled in her chest making it hard to breathe. Her wolf had come so close to the surface, and she didn't need a mirror to know her eyes were probably still glowing.

A sharp ding startled her, and the doors opened to the garage. While she didn't have her car, she didn't care. She'd walk all the way out on foot if she had to.

"Mika!"

Fuck! She turned toward the door to the stairwell just as it swung open, Delacroix bursting from behind. *He actually took six flights of stairs?* The determined look on his face as he charged toward her made her flight-or-fight response kick in, and she chose to flee. It didn't matter where she was going, she just ran in the opposite direction as fast as she could. She had a good head start, or so she thought. As a hand grasped her arm, her vision suddenly went dark. She blinked and instantly realized where she was.

"You bastard!" Her eyes adjusted quickly to the shadows as she attempted to get free of his grip. But he was too strong, like his strength was amplified here. He flipped her around so she faced him, his arm snaking around her waist.

"*Cher*, stop. Stop. *Mika.*" He backed her up until she felt something solid behind her, then pinned her arms over her head as he loomed over her. "Please."

"Why are you doing this? Just let me go."

"Oh, *cher.*" He traced a finger down her cheek. "I can't. You know I can't."

"What do you mean ..." No, she did not want to know what he meant. "Why don't you just go back to her? Seems like she doesn't mind having you close by."

He let out a chuckle. "Don't be jealous, *cher.*"

"I'm not."

"Of course you're not."

She let out an indignant squeak. "Why do you have to do that?"

"Do what?" Even in the dark she could sense his smile.

"Agree with me like that."

"You're mad because I'm agreeing with you?" he said, his tone amused. When she didn't say anything, he continued. "Mika, there's nothing going on between me and Shelby. She asked me to show her how to get out of a sleeper hold, and I said I'd think about it to be polite, but I don't plan on teaching her anything. Or even being near her if it upsets you."

"You can do whatever you want with anyone you want. I don't care. I'm not jealous."

"I don't want to do anything to anyone," he said. "Except you."

Desire sizzled through her veins. "Shut up. What are you —" She gasped when his other hand came down to cup her belly. Normally, she hated it when people even attempted to touch her pregnant belly, but now ... the warmth from his hand seeped in through all the layers of clothing she wore, and spread through her entire body.

"Mika," he gasped, his eyes wide as he stared down at her. "I ..."

She didn't know how such a simple thing could make sexual energy explode inside her, but it did.

"You want me," he said. "I can smell it."

"Hormones," she spat. "It's just hormones. And you're the closest male available to me."

In the darkness of the shadows, his eyes glowed like twin

bright stars. "Oh? And you've made use of other available males?"

She wanted to tell him yes, but bit her lip instead.

"I didn't think so."

Cocky bastard.

"Let me help you with those hormones, *cher*."

"How? By taking me to the laundromat?"

"*Non*."

Goddammit, the way he said that one word made her brain short circuit.

She shouldn't.

No, it was a bad idea.

The worst idea.

But he was offering.

"This is just sex," she said, her voice trembling. "Nothing else."

"Mm-hmm."

"And no kissing."

"Mm-hmm."

"I—" Her words died in her throat as he bent down to press his lips to her neck. The scent of damp grass, smoke, and dark sex was even more intense in the shadows, and a low growl of need escaped her mouth. "Marc, we should go back to—"

As if reading her mind, he pulled them back into the light. Her eyes shut briefly, and when she opened them again, she realized they were already by her car. "How did you do that?"

"Should I explain or drive back to The Enclave?"

"Drive."

They scrambled into the car, and she'd barely clicked her

seatbelt on when the engine roared to life. Sexual tension crackled in the air, even as they sat inches apart. Stealing a quick glance at him, she saw the look of concentration on his face as he drove, brows drawn together, lips pursed tight.

When they pulled into The Enclave, she said, "Your place."

He didn't argue, but instead, quickly turned the wheel to head toward the group of buildings that comprised the Center Cluster, maneuvering the car into the garage of one of the smaller buildings and pulled into one of the empty spots.

She followed him out to the elevators, neither speaking or touching as if doing so would break the tenuous agreement between them. When the car stopped on the fifteenth floor, he motioned for her to get out first, then led her to the apartment at the end, opening it quickly with the keys he fished out from his pocket.

When she stepped inside, she wasn't really sure what to expect. It was spacious, that's for sure, bigger than her own apartment. It was decorated comfortably in neutral colors, neither masculine or feminine, but surprisingly both at the same time. The space opened to a large living and dining area and an open kitchen. While apartments in The Enclave were subsidized, units like these were usually reserved for senior, higher-up clan members or families who need the space. She guessed there were probably two or three bedrooms in the place. How did he score this?

"I need to take care of something," he said. "Make yourself comfortable."

Before she could say anything, he disappeared down the hallway on the other side of the room. Unsure what to do, she took off her coat and scarf, then walked toward the living area and sat on the couch. She looked around; her eyes drawn to a stack of books on the coffee table.

"Huh." She picked up the heavy volume on top and read the title aloud. *"Guide to Pregnancy and Childbirth?"* Glancing back at the other books, she read the titles carefully, one by one.

What to Expect When She's Expecting

Pregnancy 101

Baby and Me

So You're Gonna Be A Dad

Her grip loosened on the book in her hand, and it landed on the carpet with a soft thud. The books looked well-thumbed through, and several pages had been dog-eared. Did Delacroix—

"Cher, is everything all right?"

Her heart jumped to her throat.

CHAPTER TWELVE

"*Cher*, is everything all right?"

Delacroix had waited for this moment to happen for what seemed like forever that when it finally did come, he realized how woefully unprepared he was. Of course, he had no idea that tonight would be the night she finally gave in, and if he had, he would have cleaned up his bedroom this morning. He had only moved into this new apartment a few days ago, and what little possessions he did have were still in boxes scattered around. He quickly tossed them into the walk-in closet and straightened out the sheets on his bed.

His question made her start, and she all but leapt off the couch. "I'm fine."

He took a step forward, watching her carefully. Had she changed her mind? Hopefully not. She clearly wanted his body; he just needed a chance to show her she also wanted the rest of him. His resolve to have her only strengthened when his hand touched her belly rounded with their pup. She and their baby were now the twin stars in his universe, shining so brightly nothing else mattered. He would kill for them, die for them. His wolf wholeheartedly agreed.

The realization made him freeze. He couldn't move, shock gripping him. So, she came to him, raising a hand to cup his cheek.

Turning his head, he nuzzled at her palm, moving lower to the pulse at her wrist, breathing in her scent. He traced his lips up her elbow to her shoulder and along her collarbone. As he moved to the soft skin of her neck, he thought to steal just one kiss from those plush lips. But no, he didn't want to scare her away, not when he was close. Besides, he knew he would have to earn that privilege, and it would be all the sweeter a victory.

"Bedroom," she gasped, and he didn't need more of an invitation than that.

He dragged her down the hallway as he continued to kiss every bit of skin he could, his fingers deftly unbuttoning the front of her blouse. As they entered his bedroom, he pushed the fabric off her shoulders and let it fall to the ground, then reached for the hook on her bra.

"Wait." She crossed her arms over her chest. "Turn off the lights first."

"But why?"

"They ... my body's changed so much." She cast her gaze downward. "You won't ... you'll find it weird."

"*Cher,*" he said gently. "Please ... don't say that."

She swallowed audibly. "Don't say I didn't warn you."

He smiled at her reassuringly, then reached behind to remove her bra. Gently, he pulled it away from her, careful not to graze at her skin, then tossed it aside. Her breasts, which had already been a handful before she got pregnant, were now fuller and heavier. And her nipples now took on a darker color, and the areola had grown much bigger.

"I told you," she said, her voice barely a whisper.

"You're right, you have changed." He lowered his head to kiss each breast. "You're even more beautiful now."

She gasped as he took a nipple into his mouth. While he was tempted to tease and bite her, instead he licked and sucked gently, increasing the pressure in increments to make sure she wasn't uncomfortable. When her breath came in short pants, he knew he'd found the sweet spot and continued the ministrations, giving each nipple equal attention.

"Marc," she moaned, digging her nails into his scalp. "I can't ..."

He lifted his head, then led her closer to the bed, just by the edge of the mattress. Kneeling down in front of her, he hooked his fingers into the waistband of her leggings and panties and pulled them all the way down, assisting her by lifting her ankles as he took them off, along with her shoes.

"So gorgeous," he murmured as he gazed up to admire her body. How could she even think he wouldn't find her attractive? Yes, her body was changing, but that didn't mean he didn't desire her. Taking one ankle in his hand, he lifted it and placed it on top of the mattress.

"What are—oh!" She braced herself on his shoulders as he moved his head between her thighs.

Her delicate pussy lips were slick with her juices, and her scent intensified, filling his nostrils and making his cock harden until it ached. He moved forward, touching his mouth to her slick cunt, gently at first to test how sensitive she was. Her flavor was subtly different than he remembered—better, more womanly—and it was driving him insane. She thrust her hips forward, and he licked and sucked at her, driving his tongue between her folds, her gasps and moans telling him what she liked. As her fingers tightened in his hair, he worked his tongue deeper, feeling her clasp around him. She mewled in disappointment when he removed his mouth, but let out a gasp when he replaced it with his fingers. His mouth closed around her clit and sucked at the delicate bud until she was screaming with her orgasm and pulling at his hair.

Before she came down from her pleasure, he maneuvered her onto the bed, making her lie back. He moved between her legs, spreading them to make room for him. "Tell me if I'm hurting you."

"You can't," she said, looking up at him with those emerald green eyes. "I just ... I need you."

Many of the pregnancy books he'd been reading in the last couple of days had sections on sex, so he tried to recall what they said. He wanted to look at her while he made love to her, so hopefully she wouldn't be uncomfortable lying on her back. Spreading her knees wider, he bent her legs and planted her feet on top of the mattress, then eased his hands under her hips to lift her up.

He took his aching cock and pressed the tip to her entrance. Slowly, he pushed in, watching her face for signs of discomfort as he filled her, and finding none, continued until he was fully in her. Watching her like this, her body so ripe and her pussy tight and hot, was making him crazy. *Not yet.* He gritted his teeth and moved tentatively.

She threw her head back and closed her eyes, lip catching in her teeth as she bit down. He moved his hands up her hips, steadying her as he gave her short thrusts, enjoying the feel of the slick and soft heat of her pussy around his cock.

"More," she urged, moving her hips up. "I'm not going to break."

Nodding, he shifted positions, and began to rock into her, working up his thrusts to a steady rhythm. "Look at me, Mika," he said through gritted teeth. "I want to see your face when you come."

She obeyed without question, staring up at him, and damn if that didn't make him want to come right then and there. He reached over to the top of her pussy, playing with the bundle of nerves until she squeezed around him, her face twisting in pleasure.

He went faster, deeper, thrusting into her with all his might. She loved it, it seemed as she met his thrusts, her eyes locking onto his as if daring him to go harder. "You want it, *cher*?"

"I—oh—yes!" Her cunt squeezed around him tighter, and he pinched her clit. "Fuck!"

He thrust all the way in. "Come, *cher*. Do it."

A cry ripped from her mouth as her body lifted off the mattress, and her thighs squeezed around him. He watched her beautiful face, her skin flushing as her orgasm spread through her, emerald eyes on him. Her pussy pulsed around him, and when she was done, he lost all control. He clutched her hips, rutting hard into her, murmuring all sorts of words in French and English that he couldn't even recall later. All he remembered was how hard he came and how drained he felt as he emptied into her.

Spent, he rolled over, staring up at the ceiling for what seemed like a long time. When the feeling returned in his legs and arms, he glanced over at her. She turned on her side, her eyes shut as her heavy breaths became slow pants. A sheen of sweat covered her gorgeous flushed skin, and his eyes immediately tracked down to her naked, swollen belly. God, he'd never seen anything more beautiful in his life. He just stared at her in wonder, a whirlwind of emotions growing inside him.

Time seemed to stretch on, but it was only minutes later when she opened her eyes. Gone was the passion-fueled look on her face. A line of worry furrowed between her brows, and her lips pursed together. "I should go," she said, rolling away from him.

I don't think so, he said to himself, but he recognized the skittish expression and body language. Even now, she was turned away from him as she scrambled around for her clothes. So instead, he climbed off the bed, picking up her discarded panties as he stood up. "Here," he said.

"Thanks." She took them from him, unwilling to meet his eyes.

"You should take a shower first," he suggested casually. "Get refreshed." His wolf protested, not wanting her to wash away their scent.

"I ... thanks." She scampered off like a rabbit, disappearing into the bathroom.

Using his keen hearing, he waited until he heard the shower turn on. After counting to five, he went in. Steam had barely fogged the enclosed shower, so he could see her curvy silhouette through the glass. His cock twitched in anticipation, ready to take her again. Moving quickly, he opened the door and slipped in.

"I—shit!" She whipped around, hand over her chest. "You scared the hell out of me. What are you—"

He reached behind her to grab the shower gel, but also

trapped her between his body and the wall. "I needed a shower too, *cher*." His eyes greedily devoured the sight of water sluicing down between her heavy breasts and over her bump.

"You could have waited," she grumbled.

"It's my shower," he pointed out. "Besides, we should conserve water, *non*?" He squirted some shower gel over her chest. "Oops, sorry."

She glared at him. "Accident?"

"Mm-hmm." His hands cupped her slick breasts, fingers teasing the sensitive nipples, making her moan aloud. Backing her against the tiled wall, he pressed his hips against her so she could feel the hardness of his cock.

"Marc, please ..." She ground up against him.

He hooked his hand under her knee and positioned between her thighs. "Yes?"

"Yes ... oh. Yes!"

———

As his senses awakened, Delacroix was immediately aware of Mika's presence all around him. The warmth of her body. The sound of the gentle rise and fall of her breath. The smell of her lavender and spice scent. The lingering taste of her skin on his tongue. And, as he opened one eye, saw her naked curves pressed up against him, the hard bump lodged against his side.

His breath caught just looking at her. Reaching down, he lay a hand on her belly, marveling at it. He could see and touch it over and over again and he would never not be amazed at the thought that life was growing inside her.

"Hmmm ..." She began to stir, her long lashes fluttering open. "What time—fuck!"

In a flurry of limbs, she scampered away from him and hopped out of bed. "What time is it?"

Glancing at the clock on his side, he said. "Eight thirty."

"Eight—Goddammit! We're already late!"

He leaned back on the headboard, watching her scramble around the room as she searched for her discarded clothes. "I think your bra's by the door, *cher*," he offered cheerfully.

That sent a death glare his way. "I should have gone back to my place last night."

He waved at the door. "No one was stopping you."

Her face turned red, then she turned her back to him to continue the hunt for her clothing. "Ha!" She raised a hand triumphantly as she found her leggings. "What are you doing still lying there like a lump? Go jump in the shower and get ready."

Smiling to himself, he rolled off the bed and strolled casually to the bathroom. While she seemed annoyed at having woken up late, she didn't completely fly off the handle and storm out by herself. There was no shame or regret at what they had done last night, and she actually wanted him to come along with her today.

Fifteen minutes later, they were in the elevator, on their way to the car. "I have a spare set of clothes at the office," she said. "If I keep my coat on until we get inside, no one will notice I'm wearing yesterday's outfit. And then—are you whistling?"

He stopped, realizing she was right. "Oh, guess I was."

The elevator stopped, and she rolled her eyes, then

strolled out before him. He merely followed; his gaze stuck on the view of her perfect ass swaying in front of him.

They made it to headquarters just after nine o'clock. She yanked the door to her office open as she unbuttoned her coat. "I can't believe you let me sleep in. Don't you have an alarm set? How do you even manage to wake up in time to get me breakfast?"

He stopped. "Uh, *cher*—"

"I shouldn't have let you talk me into staying the night." She shrugged her coat off, and nodded at his crotch. "Does your dick have some kind of magic? You better keep that thing away—"

"*Cher!*"

"What?"

He nodded in the direction of her desk. Four pairs of eyes were staring at them. Needless to say, Lizzie, Wyatt, Arch, and Cliff were much too shocked to say anything.

"Fuck. I thought this meeting was tomorrow." Color drained from her face, and she stood there, frozen. "This isn't what it looks like."

Arch let out an amused chuckle. "Really? What *does* it look like, Mika?"

Cliff's mouth pulled into a thin line. "Goddammit! You motherfucker."

Delacroix tensed as the humungous man rose to his feet and stretched out to full height. He didn't realize Cliff was especially protective of Mika. Or did the other man have feelings for her too? He was preparing for the worst when Cliff pivoted and turned toward Lizzie. "How the hell did you know we'd catch them today? Did you cheat?"

"Pay up," she laughed, which was followed by a snort, and held out her hand.

Cliff grumbled but pulled his wallet from his back pocket, took out a couple of bills, then handed them to Lizzie.

"You were betting on us?" Delacroix asked, stunned.

"Well, what else were we supposed to do?" Lizzie's eyes gleamed as she counted the bills. "Easiest money I ever made."

"If it makes you feel better, aside from us and Jacob, the pool only extended to the command floor analysts," Arch said cheerfully.

"You too, Wyatt?" Mika asked accusingly.

He shrugged. "I only bet on the first one."

"First?" Her voice rose a few decibels.

"Yeah," Lizzie said. "We were all betting on who the father was. Though that was easy to confirm, because your mom told Wyatt's mom who told my mom. And then we started betting on when—"

"Argh, stop!" Mika put up her hands. "No more betting. We have work to do, if I may remind you." Walking over to her chair, she threw her coat over the back and sat down. "Can we just get on with this meeting? I have so much stuff to do."

No one argued with her, and as they began their meeting, Delacroix slipped out. There hadn't been time to stop for breakfast this morning, so he knew she would be starving. He headed to the cafeteria and picked her up some food—oatmeal, fruits, and orange juice, but also two stacks of pancakes, a pile of bacon, an omelet with cheese and mushrooms, plus toast with butter and jam. By the time he came back with the large bag of food, the meeting had adjourned, and the four Lycans were already leaving her office.

"You have the best timing, D," Lizzie cackled. "If you had waited another day, I would have lost the bet."

"You're welcome," he said with a chuckle. "Do I get some of that cash?"

"No." She stuck her tongue out at him. "Maybe if you're good, I'll buy you lunch."

"Excuse me." Wyatt jostled his shoulder as he walked past him, a snarl under his breath.

"Thanks, *ma chouchoutte*." The pet name made Wyatt's lips tighten. "It's a date." While he wanted to see the other man's reaction, he didn't want to keep Mika waiting. Casually, he strode inside. "I have breakfast."

Her glare could have set a lesser man running in the opposing direction. "I'm not hungry."

"Of course you are. You're always hungry." He set the bag down on top of her desk. "Now, eat."

"Stop." She got up from her chair. "This ends *now*."

"What are you talking about? Don't you want breakfast?"

"I'm not talking about the damn food!" She pushed the bag from her desk, sending it to the floor. "I'm taking about *this*." Her hand waved between them. "Whatever you're doing. I told you, last night was just sex. That's *all*."

A cold fury rose in him, and he grabbed her wrists. "Stop fooling yourself, *cher*." When she tried to get out of his grasp, he only held tighter. "Mika, this may have started as sex, but it's more than that now. You know it, you just won't admit it."

"I—"

"There's been no one else but you. Not since you left. And for a while, not even before that."

He could see the internal struggle from the expression on her face so he persisted. "Last night proved this is more than just sex. Listen to your wolf, *cher*." His own wolf was all but screaming it at him. *I know, she's mine. Ours.* "It knows. Knows who I am." He dropped his voice to a whisper. "I'm your True Mate." Saying it out loud sounded so right to his ears.

"I ..." Her shoulders sagged, her head lowering. "I hardly know you."

He loosened his grip. "Then get to know me." He tipped up her chin, searching the depths of her emerald green eyes. The tightness in his chest made it difficult to breathe, but his lungs refused to work as he waited for her answer.

Her lips parted, and his heart nearly stopped when she spoke. "We're doing this backward, aren't we?" She sighed as her gaze dropped to her belly.

He could have wept in relief. "We're doing things *our way*." Moving his hand down, he placed it over the front of her bump. To his surprise, he felt something ... move? His wolf perked up, then went still. *Yes, that's our pup. Ours.* It answered with a howl of happiness.

She gasped, her hands covering his. "Did you—"

"I did," he said, in awe. Then he felt it again, the slightest bump against his palm. He then placed her hand over the same spot.

"There it is!" Her voice cracked, and her eyes became shiny with tears. "It's really ..." A sob tore from her throat. "Oh my ..."

"Yes, it's really there."

They stood there for minutes, just holding each other and her belly. The baby kicked a couple more times before it quieted down. As she brushed the tears from her face with the back of her hand, she took a deep breath. "I need some time, Marc. Don't rush me into anything I'm not ready for."

"You can have all the time you need. I promise."

"This is going too fast. I can't keep up. I don't know where this is supposed to go now."

Taking her hands in his, he kissed the inside of each one. "I don't know either, but as long as we go together, that's all that matters."

"Damned hormones," she cried, as more tears streaked down her cheeks. "This is all your fault."

A deep and genuine laugh echoed from his chest. "Whatever you say, *cher*."

CHAPTER THIRTEEN

TRUE TO HIS WORD, DELACROIX DIDN'T PUSH HER FOR more than she could give. There was no discussion on what "they" were now, though they continued on as they were. He was still a bully, though, when it came to her health. In the past two weeks, he prevented her from doing anything strenuous, not even lift her own bag or carry her lunch tray when they ate at the cafeteria. He also insisted she see the doctor right away, and even made an appointment with Dr. Blake for her himself.

"I can fill in my own name, thank you very much." Grabbing the pen and clipboard away from him, she began to fill in the blanks on the patient information form as they sat on the couch in the waiting room of the medical wing at The Enclave.

He leaned over to peer down at the paper as she finished. "You made a mistake, *cher*."

"What?" She went through every line. "I don't see any mistake."

"There." His finger landed on the space for "sex" where

she had written "F." "It's missing a few letters. M, T, W, Th—"

"Oh, ha ha." She poked him playfully with the end of the pen.

"What?" he asked innocently. "You do like it every day. And more than once—ow!" He rubbed at his arm where she jabbed him harder. "The doctor will need accurate information."

Despite his strong-arming ways, there were *some* benefits to having him around. Having sex on tap did marvelous things for her overall mood and health. She couldn't quite explain it—maybe it was the hormones, but she couldn't seem to get enough of him. Maybe he did have a magical dick, because it never failed to satisfy her, while making her want more. She couldn't decide which type of sex was better— hurried quickies in the morning, or lunchtime if they could get away—or the long, languid hours of lovemaking at night. Every night for the past two weeks, she'd stayed at his place, only going back to her apartment in the mornings to shower and change before work. No one at GI seemed to bat an eye at their ... whatever it was between them, but rather, they accepted it. *At least now they've stopped betting on us.*

"Dr. Blake will see you now, Ms. Westbrooke," the stern-looking nurse called. As she and Delacroix stood up, she frowned. "Patients only."

He looked like he wanted to protest, but she put a hand on his chest. "It's fine, it's just a routine examination." She did *not* want him in there while another male was touching her, even if Dr. Blake was a professional. Delacroix had become terribly possessive and was aggressive toward any male who came near her. The other night when they were having dinner, a waiter had accidentally touched her elbow and he nearly bit the man's head off.

"But I want to be in there with you. I want to make sure the doctor doesn't do any funny business."

"Dr. Blake is a professional and also, so old, he actually assisted in *my* birth." She rolled her eyes. "I'll have the nurse call you when it's done so you can be there during the assessment, okay?" That seemed to placate him, and he sat back down.

She went into the examination room. Dr. Blake was already there, and they proceeded with her first pre-natal exam. And as she promised, she had the nurse call Delacroix in before Dr. Blake discussed the pregnancy with her.

"Everything seems to be normal," Dr. Blake began. "For a True Mate pregnancy."

"What does that mean?" Delacroix asked, his knuckles going white as his fingers curled into fists at his sides. "Is she okay? Is the pup healthy? Will there be any complications? Pre-eclampsia? Or—"

"It means everything will be fine, Mr. Delacroix," the doctor said reassuringly. "In fact, True Mate females have the healthiest pregnancies I've ever seen. "

The look of relief on his face was evident. "And when do we know if it's a boy or girl?"

"When it's born." Dr Blake looked at her when Delacroix seemed taken aback.

"I'm afraid he's not familiar with True Mate pregnancies, Doctor." She turned to him. "While the baby makes me invulnerable to any harm, it also blocks my body from any type of invasive examination. Sonograms, X-rays, not even an

MRI machine can penetrate whatever magical shield is around me."

"Even now, we don't know the reason why," Dr. Blake continued. "We tried doing some studies and experiments on ways to examine True Mate fetuses over thirty years ago. Dr. Jade Creed, our leading Lycan scientist who studies magic, tried different methods, even magical ones, but to no avail."

"Then how do you know the pup is healthy?"

"Every True Mate child I've witnessed being born or delivered myself has come into this world one hundred percent healthy," he stated.

"Every one?" He sounded skeptical.

"Yes, since the first one in the last century." The doctor gestured to Mika. "See for yourself."

Delacroix's brows wrinkled in confusion.

Dr. Blake frowned. "You really have no idea?"

"I haven't told him." She lay a hand on top of his. "It's me. He's talking about me. I was the first True Mate baby born in a very long time. I was told that up until I was conceived, True Mates were thought to be a legend."

He looked flummoxed. "I didn't know, *cher*."

Of course not, seeing as they never talked of anything about their past. She'd never even told him about—

"Are you all right, Ms. Westbrooke? You suddenly seem pale."

Delacroix's dark eyes narrowed at her. "I thought you said pregnant True Mates were healthy, doctor?"

"I'm fine," she managed to say. "Just ... felt fatigued."

The rest of the appointment seemed to go by in a haze. Dr. Blake talked about her progress and her due date, but it all went over her head. All she could think about was *Joe*.

Had she completely forgotten about him? Of course not. He had been her husband. Nothing was going to change that. But a pit formed in her stomach when she thought of Delacroix. He had no idea about Joe, and she didn't know how to tell him. Should she casually mention it? No, the time for that had passed. Maybe she should sit him down ... and tell him what?

"Are you sure you're okay, *cher*?" he asked as they left the doctor's office.

"I ... I'm fine."

He moved closer to her, bending his head, then stopped. As if her guilt wasn't bad enough, her no-kissing rule was another thing that made her feel even worse. Despite all the ways they shared their bodies, they hadn't kissed since the first time. He hadn't pressed her, though she could see it was bothering him.

She did want him to kiss her, but it just felt so intimate, as if there was this invisible line between no kissing and kissing, and the moment she crossed it, she feared there was no going back. That it would mean she really would have to move on and forget Joe.

"If you don't feel well, we don't have to go out tonight."

"Tonight?" Her head whipped toward him.

"Yes, tonight. Your father's birthday party. Alynna asked me to remind you."

Oh crap.

Mika wasn't sure how her mother had gotten wind of what was going on—though knowing Alynna, it wasn't a surprise—but she had invited Delacroix along to Alex's birthday party at their apartment that night. All her siblings were going to be there as well, and it would be the first time they would meet Delacroix and see them together. She couldn't miss it; no, she couldn't do that to her father, but if the subject of Joe came around, then she didn't know what to do. So, as a precaution, she called her mother before they headed over to their place while Delacroix was in the shower.

"You haven't told him?" Alynna asked incredulously. "Sweetie, why not? You shouldn't be afraid—"

"I'm not afraid," she bit out. "It's just ..." How could she explain it to her mother, when she couldn't understand it herself? "Please, just tell everyone? Make some excuse. Tell them it'll upset me."

Alynna let out a long sigh. "All right, but you have to tell him about Joe soon. Before he finds out from someone else."

Though she'd been nervous the entire dinner, no one in her family breathed a word about Joe. It probably wasn't difficult though, because he wasn't a subject they spoke about often. Truth was, since he died, everyone seemed to walk on eggshells around her, afraid to upset her. She also realized that she'd missed them all and that she'd been pushing her parents, sister, and brothers away for the last two years. This was the first time she could recall they'd been together that they all seemed at ease.

"Were you worried about your family not approving of me?" Delacroix asked as they walked back to his apartment when the dinner party ended.

"Huh? Not at all. They adored you." Of course they did; Delacroix could charm the pants off anyone. Her father seemed to accept him, while her mother was delighted by his flattery. Nathan and Knox developed a natural camaraderie with him as they chatted about sports and beer, while the normally shy and reserved Amanda chatted amiably with him.

"Then what were you all jittery about the whole evenin'?"

"I—" It was on the tip of her tongue. To tell him. *Do it now.* "Nothing." She really was a coward.

He looked like he wanted to press the matter, but hesitated. "So," he looped her arm through his as they continued walking, "when do I get to see the baby photos your mother promised?"

She threw her head back and laughed. "How about ... never?"

He continued to tease her, making her feel at ease and forgetting about her worries. Still, in the back of her mind, it hung there—that big secret she was keeping from him. *Tomorrow*, she told herself as she held on tighter to him. *I'll tell him tomorrow.*

———

Mika really was trying hard to tell him, but there never seemed to be the right time. The truth weighed on her mind, and it was like waiting for the shoe to drop, but every time she worked up the courage, she just found one excuse after the other to delay it.

Plus of course, she still had a job to do, and this week seemed to be when shit hit the fan. The mages had attacked two of their allies, one in Ohio, and the other in Mexico City. While there were no casualties, it only spooked the other clans they were in talks with. Julianna had reported that three of them had already canceled meetings.

"I'll do my best to get them back on track," Julianna said via videoconference. Aside from the envoys, Daric had joined them as well, and he sat next to Mika in her office.

"Dublin's mighty scared, but I'll work on O'Leary," Duncan added.

"Thank you, Duncan." Mika said. "I'm sorry this has made your job harder."

"Don't worry about us," Julianna said. "But, do you have any more intelligence about these attacks? I mean, specifics. What did the mages want? Did they take anything or anyone?"

Mika had been asking herself the same thing, ever since the mages came back into the picture. But there was no pattern they could discern or specific demands from the mages. "No, I'm afraid we don't know anything new."

"Isn't it strange?" Duncan's brows knitted together. "All these attacks over the past year ... and we still don't know what they want exactly."

"They want the artifacts, and they want to destroy us, that we know for sure." Mika said.

"Yes, but all they need is the former to do the latter," Duncan added. "What do you think, Daric?"

The warlock's turquoise eyes grew dark. "You're right. The mages only came to us because we had the dagger and Adrianna and Lucas. Then we started our campaign against them, and so we thought they were only retaliating for what we did. But now ... their targets seem random but the mages are so organized that they must have some plan. They can't possibly be doing this just to prevent us from gaining more alliances."

"And then there was that attack against you, Mika,"

Julianna pointed out. "It was specific, almost personal, don't you think?"

Her jaw dropped. She hadn't thought of that, but somehow, it made sense that it would be a personal attack. But who would want her dead?

"There was something off about the whole thing," Daric said. "I've been too busy to investigate myself, but it seems like an anomaly. Has there been any other progress on the investigation? Do we know the identity of the assassin or who hired them?"

"I'm afraid not," she said with a shake of her head. "A total dead end." But now that they pointed out how unusual the attack was, she couldn't help but think about it. "There's not much more to talk about," she said to Julianna and Duncan. "You should get some rest before your flight back to New York. We can continue in person once you're back."

They said their goodbyes, and Mika hung up the call. "What do you think, Daric? About all this?"

He rose from his chair. "I think ... I have a gut feeling that your assassin isn't connected to all this."

"It's not? But then, who could have sent them? My only real enemies are the mages. You know I haven't had much of a life outside GI."

"I don't know." His mouth tensed into a grim line. "But I will do my best to find out."

"If it's not the mages then you shouldn't bother—no, don't worry about me. So far, no one's tried to attack me again."

"Still, it's a good thing you have your protector with you." There was something about his tone that sounded like he wasn't surprised about her and Delacroix. "He will ensure nothing happens to you, so I'm glad to leave you in his hands."

A thought popped into her head. Were those rumors about the warlock true? "Daric, did you see—" But before she could finish her question, he disappeared. *How convenient.*

"*Cher.*" The door opened, and Delacroix poked his head inside her office. "All done for the day?" He walked over to her and placed his hands on her shoulders, the contact never failing to make her feel calm. "Why don't we leave early tonight? It's the weekend, you really shouldn't be working."

"I can't rest with all the stuff that's going on. You know that—oh!" She moaned as his fingers began to massage the knots in her neck. "Yes ... don't stop."

"You know I don't," he chuckled. "I heard you complaining this morning to your mother that your clothes don't fit right anymore."

"Yes, please remind me how I'm *fat*," she said glumly.

"*Non*, that's not why I said that. Do not try to start a fight, *cher*." He muttered something in French under his breath. "You are beautiful, and I want you now more than ever." There was a gleam of possession in his eyes as he placed a hand over her growing belly. "But you need to be comfortable. How about we go shopping, and you can get some new clothes, then we get some dinner? Anything you like."

"Anything?"

"Absolutely."

"All right." She grabbed her purse from the back of the chair and walked over to her closet so she could take her coat out. "But dinner first. I want two racks of barbecue ribs to myself, French fries, a baked potato with everything on it, cornbread and honey butter, plus two desserts. If you try to take a bite, I'm going to stab you in the eye with my fork."

He laughed. "I value my life far too much, *cher*."

———

Not surprisingly, she did feel better after food. After her humungous dinner, they went to a popular department store in Midtown so she could get some new maternity clothes. Delacroix seemingly had the patience of a saint as he waited for her outside the dressing room, never complaining as she tried on outfit after outfit. She ended up with two large bags of clothing which he grabbed from the cashier.

"I'm pooped," she declared as they walked out of the maternity section. "Can we go now, please?"

"Wait." He stopped, then nodded to the display on the right. It was a nursery set-up with a crib, changing table, and rocking chair, all decorated with a circus animal theme. "Let's stop in there for a couple of minutes."

"Oh." God, she hadn't even thought of where the baby would sleep. The birth seemed so far away in her mind. "I don't have to worry about it for a while."

He took her hands in his and kissed each one. "*Cher*, I've been thinking."

She tried to sound as casual as she could. "Oh? About what?"

"You know, we're runnin' out of time, and the baby will be here soon."

"I have plenty of time."

"*We* have less than four months, according to Dr. Blake," he said. "With all the trouble brewin', you won't have much time to prepare, and I know your work is important. I could never ask you to give it up."

"Oh." *Thank God.*

"So, I want to make it easier for you. Move in with me."

Now *that*, she didn't expect. "M-m-move in?"

"You practically live at my apartment," he pointed out. "You only go home to change your clothes, and you won't keep anything more than a toothbrush at my place."

She crossed her arms over her chest. "I have too much stuff. I don't want to clutter your place. I know guys can be sensitive about that."

"Most guys, yes, but you haven't asked me if I minded?"

She bit her lip, unable to answer him.

"Why do you think I asked to be moved to a larger apartment? Mika, if it's not obvious by now, then let me say it: I want you to be with me. You and the baby. For us to be a fam—"

"Don't push me!" She yanked her hands away. Panic had set in and her emotions were starting to spin out of control. "You said you'd give me time. It's only been two weeks."

"How much time then, Mika?" He rubbed his hand down his face. "When will you let me in? At least a little bit. Leave a crack in the door so I can take a peek. Tell me what's been bothering you. I know there's something you've been keeping from me."

"Oh, and I suppose you've been open with me all this time?" She shot back. "Do you want to tell me the real story of that night you called Nick to get you the hell out of that Podunk town? Why you left the clan who took you in when you were orphaned?"

His mouth clamped shut, and his eyes flashed with anger.

"I'll get the car," he said in a robotic tone. "Wait for me outside."

She knew she had made a mistake. "Marc. Marc!" But he didn't stop or even turn back. As his figure retreated, she could only watch, helpless. The pit in her stomach was growing. It was wrong to say those things to him when he'd been nothing but patient with her. She should have been open from the beginning.

Though she was still feeling numb, she somehow found her way to the street level. They had parked about a block away, so he would likely pull up to the front entrance of the department store. As she stood at the exit, keeping her eye out for her car, she heard someone call her name.

"Mika?"

She turned around, and it took seconds before her brain put together the identity of the owner of the voice. "Madeline?" Her heart stopped for one beat as she stared at the white-haired, older woman before her and the man beside her. "George?"

"I thought that was you." Achingly familiar blue eyes looked back at her.

"I'm ..." There were no words to describe how she felt, except it was like a phantom pain that had resurfaced. Because what was she supposed to say to Madeline and George Morgan, Joe's parents. "H-how have you both been?"

Madeline looked at her with a curious expression, then her eyes dropped lower. "Oh." There was a hitch in her voice as she stared at Mika's obviously pregnant belly. "You're ..." She swallowed audibly. "Congratulations."

Mika didn't miss the brief pain that passed across the older woman's face. After all, Madeline knew the struggles she and Joe had, about how hard they tried for a baby of their own. And, of course, now she must think—

George cleared his throat and put an arm around his wife. "Mika, dear, it's lovely to see you. I'm glad to see you're well." He tightened his hold on his wife. "We both are, aren't we Maddy?"

"Oh." Madeline blinked, as if she's been shaken out of a trance. "*Oh!* Dear." She shook her head. "It's been a long while and we didn't really keep in touch as much as we should have ... I was just caught by surprise."

"I should have told you," Mika said bitterly. "It was ... insensitive of me to spring this on you like this."

Madeline looked horrified. "Oh no, please don't think that, Mika." Her hands, paper-thin and wrinkled, squeezed around hers with a reassuring strength. "You'll always be like a daughter to us. But you also have your own life, we all do. And we must ... move on." She looked to her husband, giving him a weak smile to which he replied with a solemn nod. "Not to ever forget Joe and what he means to us, but also continue on with our lives because that's what he would have wanted." She gave Mika's hands a squeeze. "I'm so happy to see you've fulfilled your dream of being a mother. He would have wanted this for you. And I'm sure your husband must be very happy too."

"I—" How to say it? How to tell them? "I don't—"

"*Cher?*"

And there it was, the sound of the other shoe dropping.

She'd been so caught up with Madeline and George that she didn't hear the car approach or Delacroix coming up to her. She wished she had talked to him about Joe before, but now it was too late. Unless she quickly got him out of here and then explain to him. Really explain this time.

Madeline smiled warmly. "Oh, hello. Is this your—"

"Bodyguard," she said, the tone coming out flat. Without even looking at him, she felt Delacroix flinch at the word. Her wolf didn't like that and clawed at her in anger.

George didn't look convinced. "Oh. You're still working at the security firm at your uncle's company?"

"Kind of," she said. "I've moved departments. Promotion."

"That's nice—Oh no." Madeline looked at her watch. "George, they're going to give our table away if we don't hurry."

"You're right, Maddy. We should go. Mika," he began. "It's nice seeing you."

"Please, call me anytime, you know our number at home," Maddy said, the corner of her eyes crinkling as she smiled. "Congratulations." She reached over to wrap her arms around Mika.

"Th-thank you," she murmured as her former mother-in-law hugged her tight. "I might take you up on that."

"I would love it."

She watched as the couple crossed the street, her own heart thudding her rib cage. "Marc, I—"

He quickly turned around without saying anything, but the stiffness in his shoulders and his tightly controlled gait told her *everything*.

I fucked up.

Her wolf agreed, its claws sinking into her. And she allowed it, because it couldn't compare to the pain she'd inflicted on him.

I have to make it right!

He had already slipped inside the car, and she scrambled after him. "Marc—"

The engine roared to life as he turned the key in the ignition. Before she could continue, he stepped on the gas, making the car jerk forward. She braced herself on the dash, then quickly secured herself with the seatbelt.

From the grim set of his jaw and the tension in his arms and shoulders, she knew this wasn't the time to talk. So, she sank back into her seat and clamped her mouth shut as the car made its way uptown.

When they got to The Enclave, she realized he wasn't driving toward his apartment building, but to hers. Her heart sank as the car entered the garage and pulled up to the front of the elevator lobby. Wordlessly, he got out of the car, took her packages out of the trunk, and came to the front to open the door for her.

"What are you doing?" she asked.

"I'm escorting you to your apartment, Ms. Westbrooke." Each word cut into her like a blade.

"Marc, please." She got out of the car and faced him. "Don't be like this."

"Like what?" He kept his stare ahead, his eyes hard as flint.

"Like you're ... like you're just—"

"Your bodyguard?" he finished. "Or some guy you fuck when you're feeling horny?"

"No! No, Marc, please." She gripped his arms. "It's not like that. You're not just some guy. I'm sorry I said that to ... to ..."

"Are you ashamed of me? Ashamed to tell your fancy

friends who I am?" He wrenched himself away from her. "I never thought it would ever matter to me what other people think, only your opinion mattered. But now I see the truth. I'm not good enough for you, I never was," he spat. "I'm just poor bayou trash. My own parents didn't want—"

"Stop." His words made her ache. Ache for him, for what had happened to him. And what she had done to him. It was time to lay things out in the open. "I don't see you that way, please. How can you think I do?"

"Then why won't you let me in?"

"Because ... because." Her throat was burning, but she pushed on. "Because it feels like if I do, I'm betraying *him!*" The words shocked her, but it was what she needed to admit. Moving on felt like a betrayal to Joe.

His brows furrowed in confusion. "Who?"

She had practiced this so many times in her head. What she would say to him, how to explain. But really, how else could she tell him? "Joe. He was my husband."

"Was?" He looked shocked. "You were ..."

She nodded. "He's ... gone."

"I ..." He raked his hands through his hair. "How did he ...?"

"It was a car accident. We were on our way home, and a drunk driver crashed into us. I s-s-survived because of my Lycan healing. He was killed on impact. I—" She drew in a deep breath as he embraced her and the tears began to flow. "I'm sorry I didn't tell you earlier."

"*Shh ... cher.*" He loosened his grip on her. "Was that couple you were talking to—"

"His parents. I was just as surprised to see them as they were to run into me. After the funeral, we said we'd keep in touch and never did. I know they were shocked when they saw I was pregnant. They said they were happy for me, and I know they were because that's the kind of people they are. But I just didn't want to rub it in their faces that I ... we ..." she sobbed. "That I had moved on and was having my own child while they had lost theirs."

"Mika." He soothed her back with his hand. "It's all right, *cher*. You don't have to explain. And you don't have to be sorry for not telling me earlier. It's a difficult subject for you to talk about."

"It is, but it was wrong of me to keep that from you. I just ... I wasn't ready." She took a deep breath. "It was just sex in the beginning. But it's so much more now. You're so much more. You're my True Mate." His hand stopped mid stroke. She wanted to say so many things to him, reassure him too. But she couldn't say it, not yet. So instead, she decided to show him. "Kiss me," she whispered.

His head bent down to her neck, but before his mouth could make contact with her skin, she cupped his face and stopped him. "No. Kiss *me*."

Dark eyes flashed with emotion before he bent down to press his lips to her. It was just the gentlest pressure, like he was afraid that she would disappear or shatter into pieces if he kissed her too hard. When she arched up against him, he deepened the kiss, and his arms wound around her to hold her close, her bump cradled between them.

His tongue slid past her lips and teeth, tasting her mouth, coaxing her to open up to him. Before long he was ravaging her mouth, his kisses hungry like he'd been starved for days.

She didn't know how long they'd been kissing, but when they both finally pulled back, she had to brace herself against him. She'd never been kissed like that, and from the look on his face, this was probably a first for him too. He still held her, one hand around her and the other protectively covering her belly. "Let's go back to my apartment."

"No," she said, placing her hands over his. "Let's go back to *our* place."

He let out a low, pleased growl and nodded.

CHAPTER FOURTEEN

MOVING MIKA INTO HIS APARTMENT TOOK LESS TIME and effort that actually convincing her to do it. Though Delacroix had seen some glimpses of her place here and there in the last few weeks, he'd never actually been inside. So, he was surprised to find the place practically bare, with only the furniture the management provided and no personal knickknacks or decorations. They only had to pack her clothes and bathroom toiletries, which took most of an afternoon. When he asked where the rest of her things were, she shrugged.

"I have personal items in those"—she pointed her chin at the boxes in the living room—"and some stuff from when I was in school are with my parents, in my childhood bedroom. And the rest, well ... I gave to Goodwill or sold along with the Brooklyn house."

The house she had shared with her husband.

It still sometimes floored him to know that she had been married, but not in a bad way. There was a twinge of jealousy there, but there would always be that emotion when it came to her and anyone she'd been involved with. However, it was the idea someone had loved her first that would always make him feel uneasy.

But truly, what amazed him was her strength and courage, and her ability to get up every day and live her life after her husband died. Frankly, he didn't think he could do the same. Losing Mika would destroy him, because he loved her so much, he couldn't bear the thought of taking a breath without her.

The thought that he loved her had come so easy to him, and yet he hadn't said anything to her. There was still some fear, that she wouldn't feel the same way. But surely, she must at least feel strongly for him. She let him kiss her now, meaning she didn't fear intimacy. She opened up to him too. It stuck in his craw, though, that she hadn't said anything concrete about her feelings. Would she try to run again? Or put her walls up? Was this just the calm before the storm?

Maybe she was waiting for him. Or waiting for him to open up about his past. She already knew most of it, but the thought of her knowing *everything* made his stomach drop to his knees. Would she look at him the same way if she really knew the things he'd done in the past, what he'd done that *night*?

"God, I'm going to tear my hair out," Mika said glumly. She was sitting at her desk, face scrunched up in concentration.

"What's wrong, *cher*?" Since they had moved in together two weeks ago, there really was no need to hide their relationship or pretend they were strictly professional, so any time he wasn't helping Cliff and Jacob with training, he spent inside her office.

"Sorry, tech problems." She picked up the phone. "Lizzie, I know you've got a lot on your plate, but I need you up here ... okay, great. Thanks."

He walked over to her and placed his hands on her shoulders, slowly beginning to massage the muscles there. "Relax, it's just a computer. No need to work yourself up."

"Mmmm." She closed her eyes and leaned into him. "That feels good. Maybe we can lock the door ..."

"Oh?" Now this was intriguing.

"And then we can close the blinds ..."

"Go on." He kneaded a particularly stubborn knot, making her moan so deliciously.

"And I can take off ..."

God, thinking about her naked and bent over her desk was enough to make him hard. "Yes?"

"My shoes ..."

"And what else?"

"My socks." She looked up at him, eyes all soft and doe-like. "And then you can massage my feet."

"Massage your—" He smirked at her. "Oh, ha ha, funny. But I bet you won't be laughing when I take you over my knee and spank your—"

"All right, what's the problem?" Lizzie breezed in, not bothering to knock. Today she was dressed in a bright pink cut-off sweater that showed off her belly button ring, a short black velvet skirt, leggings, and thigh-high boots.

"It's my computer, it's freezing again. Among other things."

It wasn't surprising that Mika was more tense than usual. In the last two weeks, there had been one more attack—this time, in New Jersey. The mages had hit the headquarters of the Corvinus family, injuring many of the Lycans there. No one had died, but they had burned half the compound. Mika was working overtime, trying to find out how the mages infiltrated the Corvinus compound and surprise them in the middle of the day.

Lizzie was already working her magic on Mika's computer, her hand going to the CPU tower. "Ah, okay." She pursed her lips as her head bobbed up and down, as if she was a doctor listening to a patient. "Gotcha. Graphics card needs an update," she said to Mika. "I'll take care of it."

"Thanks, Liz."

"You know," she began, perching her hip on the side of the desk, "Things have been really busy around here, and I'm sure you're probably stressed as fuck. You should maybe, do something fun. Relax. Blow off some steam."

"I can't take any time off," Mika said. "There's too much—"

"I'm not talking about a vacay, Mika." She tapped her finger on her chin. "Oh! Before you called I was on my way out. Jacob and I are going to check out the Winter Carnival at Brooklyn Bridge Park. Our brother, Anthony, and his wife and kid are going to be there. You guys should come."

"I don't—"

"Sounds like a good idea," Delacroix interrupted. Some fun would definitely benefit his mate. When Mika opened her mouth, he silenced her protest with a hand. "C'mon, *cher*. It's nearby, just across the bridge. You can take your dinner break. I bet there'll be popcorn, corndogs, hot chocolate, pretzels, and other junk food you shouldn't be having."

The promise of food seemed to be enough to coax Mika along, so she agreed, and they all bundled up and headed out.

As they walked out of the elevator and into the garage, they passed Wyatt in the hallway.

"Come join us, *mon ami*," Delacroix said. "It will be fun."

Wyatt's eyes flickered to Lizzie briefly, and he seemed to consider it. "I have to work late tonight," he said in a tight voice. "I'll see you all later." Without another word, he walked past them.

Lizzie shrugged. "Maybe he's too busy playing with the stick up his ass."

"All work and no play make Wyatt a dull boy," Jacob snickered. "I'll race you to the car, Liz! Last one's a rotten egg." He dashed across the garage.

"Hey! No fair!" Lizzie ran after him as Jacob taunted her all the way to the row of parked vehicles at the end of the garage.

Delacroix sighed. "She really doesn't see it, does she?"

"See what?" Mika asked.

"Wyatt." He nodded at the other Lycan, who was standing by the elevator. "He's got it bad for her."

"Lizzie?" she said incredulously. Her head whipped to Wyatt, then back to the female, who had hopped onto Jacob's back and was pulling on her brother's hair. "And Wyatt?"

"Yeah. Good Lord, am I the only one seeing this?" he said in an exasperated tone. "Maybe I should start a betting pool."

She opened her mouth to say something, but the roar of an engine cut her off. "C'mon losers!" Jacob shouted as he stuck his head out the driver's side window. "Get in!"

And so, twenty minutes later, they found themselves at Brooklyn Bridge Park, which had been transformed into a winter wonderland. Lights and decorations littered around the park, along with large ice sculptures. Stalls with people selling delicious-smelling food and drinks lined up one side of the park, while booths selling knickknacks and games of chance were set up on the other. They met up with Lizzie's brother and his family at the glass-enclosed Jane's Carousel at the end of the park, as they were in line to take a ride. Mika seemed to know the family well and introduced Delacroix.

"Nice to meet you." Anthony Martin shook his hand firmly, his white teeth stark against his tawny skin as he smiled. It wasn't just that he looked vastly different from Lizzie and Jacob that told Delacroix he was obviously adopted, but it was the fact that he was completely human. "This is Blaise." He nodded to the little toddler perched on his hip, her face buried in her father's shoulder. "She's a little shy around strangers, sorry about that."

"I'm Hannah." The blonde woman next to him smiled brightly. "It's nice to finally meet you, Delacroix. I've heard so much about you."

"You have?"

"We're related, kind of," Mika said. "Hannah's father is Dante Muccino, who is my Uncle Grant's brother-in-law. If you go to Muccino's and *Petit Louve* a lot, then you've probably met her brothers, Gio and Dominic, who run those restaurants."

Like Anthony, Hannah was also human, so she must be another adopted relative or one of her parents was not a Lycan. "Oh, I understand. Nice to meet you, Hannah."

"Oops, the line's moving." Anthony ushered his wife forward. "We've been waiting forever, so we better get moving. Blaise has been looking forward to this all day."

"We'll see you later!" Hannah said as she waved at them.

"I'm hungry," Jacob moaned. "Let's go get something to eat."

"I can get with that," Mika said as they headed out into the cold and toward the row of vendors.

"I want two of everything," Jacob said, his eyes greedily looking at the various booths they passed.

"And I'll have two of that—hey, where's Lizzie?" Mika glanced around. "She was right behind us."

It seemed they had lost their companion in the throng of people that had suddenly appeared. Despite the cold temperatures and the bitter cold wind whipping across the shore, the Winter Carnival was packed, probably because a famous band was going to put on a concert on the main stage.

Jacob had somehow snagged a hotdog and was stuffing it into his mouth. "I dunno," he said between bites. "But she's got a horrible sense of direction. Has this tendency to walk around in circles." He swallowed and wiped his mouth with a napkin. "I'm not surprised she's lost. Don't worry, she'll turn up."

"Can we get some food please?" Mika said, her eyes growing wide as someone with a large pretzel walked past them.

"All right, but stick close to me, okay?" Delacroix tightened his hold around her. "I don't want to lose you too."

They stopped at almost every vendor, though the crush of people was preventing them from staying in one spot for too long. Mika already had two hotdogs, a plate of deep-fried chocolate cookies, and nachos when she whined for hot chocolate.

"But we already passed that booth," he said in an exasperated voice.

"Please?" She pouted and put her hand over her belly.

He slapped a hand on his forehead. "All right, *cher*. But we have to turn back. Hang on to me ..." Her grip tightened around his arm and she nodded.

Despite the throng of people, he managed to turn around and walk back toward the hot chocolate vendor. When he finally reached it, he turned back to Mika. "Which one—Mika?"

His heart stopped. She wasn't behind him as he'd thought. He had been so busy trying to move through the crowd that he didn't feel her hand slipping away. Scanning further behind, he didn't see any sign of her. It was also too noisy, and there were too many scents in the air to try and follow her trail. "Mika!" he shouted over the sea of people. "Mika!"

She's fine, he told himself. The crush got too much for her, and she was probably standing somewhere, getting some air. He waded through the crowd and ended up on a grassy patch behind the hotdog vendor's stall. His eyes scanned the area, but there was no sign of her. Where was she?

Movement from the corner of his eye caught his attention. When he turned to follow it, he saw something in the distance—a pair of blue eyes glowing in the bushes.

No! Blood roared in his ears as he lunged forward. A very large, dark shape darted from the bushes and into the street. There was no mistaking it. It was a Lycan, and one that he knew all too well.

He chased it for two blocks, through the streets of trendy DUMBO until the Manhattan Bridge loomed overhead. The massive wolf stopped and turned around; teeth bared at him.

"Nice of you to join us, Delacroix. *Ça va?*"

He ground his teeth and turned around toward the source of the voice. "Alphonse?"

Alphonse Broussard's mouth curled up into a cruel smile. "Hello, *mon ami*. Surprised to see me?"

Shock coursed through his system. What was the Beta of Pont Saint-Louis doing in New York?

"He don't look too happy now, though." Another figure emerged from the shadows, this time, a female with short blonde hair and cold blue eyes.

"Should I be, Zeline?" he mocked. "You're in violation of Lycan law, showing up here without permission from Lucas Anderson." Laws prevented Lycans from going into another clan's territory without going through the proper channels.

"Fuck Lycan law," Alphonse spat.

"You would risk your freedom and Remy's wrath? You know he'd get in big trouble with the Lycan High Council."

"Fuck them too," Alphonse said. "Don't tell me you've gone soft, *mon ami*, bending over for the 'high and mighty' council."

"They don't care about us and we don't care about them," Zeline spat.

"What the fuck do you want, then?" *And what were they doing here?* "Ah, of course. Remy's still sending you to do his dirty work."

A tick in the Beta's jaw pulsed. "He sent us to take care of you."

"Is he pissed about the transfer? That was over a year ago. I know teenagers who've gotten over their first love faster than that."

"Still a smart ass, eh?" Alphonse said. "Maybe you'll learn your place once we teach you a lesson."

His muscles coiled with tension, ready to spring. "Three"—he counted the Lycan in wolf form whom he recognized as Jean-Baptiste, another of his former clan mates —"against one, doesn't seem fair. For you guys I mean." He quickly assessed the shadows around them, figuring out how to hop from one to another so he could deliver the most damage. Did Alphonse forget how his powers worked? He was an idiot, choosing this place to confront Delacroix.

"Not so fast, *mon ami*." Alphonse gestured with a nod. "Wait until you see who we got."

From afar, he could see a large figure approaching them whom he recognized as Thibault Fontenot, a huge and mean *sonofabitch* who carried out Broussard's dirty work. He was dragging someone along, a female, from the silhouette.

Oh no. *Mika*. His chest tightened. They had her!

His wolf let out an angry, guttural sound and raked its claws against his skin. He forced it to remain calm. "If you've hurt her—"

"Get your filthy hands off me, you motherfucker!"

What?

While the voice was familiar, it was not Mika.

"I swear, I'm going to rip your balls off and make you eat them," Lizzie screamed as Thibault hauled her forward. "What—Delacroix?" Her eyes went wide. "What's going on?"

The relief he felt that it wasn't Mika they'd snatched was short-lived. In fact, a part of him almost wished it was Mika, because his mate was not only trained in combat, but was also invulnerable to any harm. Lizzie, on the other hand, was neither, and while she was a Lycan, any of his former clan mates could rip her to shreds before she could even shift.

"Let her go." He focused his gaze at Alphonse. "Remy wants me? Fine, I'll come with you. But she has nothing to do with ... us."

"Gone soft for a bit of trim, have you?" Alphonse laughed. "I always thought you were a tough one, Delacroix. You even survived a goddamn bullet to the chest."

His jaw hardened. So, Remy had sent the assassin for him? What the fuck was going on? "If you hurt her—"

"What will you do?"

He whipped around, and saw the wolf that had led him here had transformed back into its human form. Jean-Baptiste cracked his neck. "Does the carpet match the drapes?" He asked as he leered at Lizzie. "Mm-mmm, I've got an *envie* for some strawberry pie."

Lizzie let out an outraged roar, but Thibault restrained her and placed a large hand over the lower half of her face. Her eyes filled with hate as she struggled against the giant, though to no avail as he kept his hold tight.

"I'll do whatever you want," Delacroix said. "I won't fight ... just let her go." He knew what his former clan mates were capable of and wouldn't put it past them to hurt Lizzie. And that sick bastard Jean-Baptiste had a well-earned reputation for hurting women; he even bragged about it.

"Oh, you will, Delacroix," Alphonse sneered. "You'll do anything we want. Don't even try your little trick, because the moment you disappear, Thibault will snap her pretty neck."

"Take me away then," he said. "Restrain me. Lock me up. Do what you want."

"You bet we—"

A bright, burning light streaking between them followed by a large explosion made Alphonse jerk back in surprise.

Jacob!

As another fireball streaked across the air, Delacroix knew he only had seconds to react, and he stepped back, melted into the shadow, then reappeared behind Alphonse to grab his arms and toss him clear across the street. He hit the side of a brick building with a large crash.

Glancing around, he saw Jacob was taking on Thibault, his flaming hands waving the giant away. Lizzie was on the ground, struggling to get to her feet when a wolf—Jean-Baptiste, who had shifted again—lunged at her, raking its claws down her back. She let out a blood-curdling scream.

"Lizzie!" He was about to run to her when another Lycan stepped into his path. Zeline's she-wolf snapped its gigantic jaws at him, daring him to come.

Fuck. He hadn't shifted yet, as it would take time and leave him vulnerable, and Zeline would surely take advantage of such an opening. His best chance of survival would be to run into the shadows and get away. But Jean-Baptiste had Lizzie pinned down on the ground, so that wasn't an option.

Before he could act, a large, dark blur whizzed in front of him, knocking the female away. Two wolves rolled on the ground in a tangle of teeth, claws, and fur. The scent of lavender and spice wafted into his nose as he realized who the other wolf was, and his own wolf urged him to help their mate.

No, we have to trust her. Though his chest tightened, he knew Mika could hold out against Zeline. It was Lizzie he had to worry about, so he charged toward her. Jean-Baptiste was still on top of her, so he used his momentum to knock him away, then grabbed Lizzie and pulled her into the shadows. He carried her as far away as he could, emerging in the parking lot across the street, and lay her gently against the side of a parked van. "Stay still, Lizzie," he said. "You'll be fine."

Her face was pale, but she managed a nod and raised her hand, gesturing to her smart watch. "Called. Jacob," she stuttered. "And backup."

"Good girl." He gave her a quick kiss on the forehead. "I'll be right back, *ma chouchoutte.*"

He retraced his steps through the shadows, and back under the bridge. To his relief, more New York Lycans had arrived, and he saw Arch hauling a once again human Jean-Baptiste to his feet and taking him toward one of the GI vans. Meanwhile, Cliff and Jacob had Thibault restrained with special reinforced handcuffs. But where was—

"Marc!"

The sound of Mika's voice made him want to weep with relief. Turning around, he saw her running toward him, wrapped up in a coat that was several sizes too big. She hurtled toward his open arms. "*Cher.*" His voice hitched in his throat, and he realized he was shaking. "I was so scared." His hands immediately moved down to her belly. *Thank you for taking care of mama.*

"It's all right," she soothed. "I'm fine. No injuries whatsoever, and I handed that bitch's ass back to her."

"I didn't doubt you for a second," he said with a weak smile.

"I got lost in the crowd, and I went looking for you. Then I got a message from Lizzie. Sent it to the entire team, telling us what was happening. We tracked you down here."

"Lizzie!" He glanced back toward the parking lot. "I took her away, but she's hurt."

Mika's eyes widened. "Let's go get her."

They were crossing the street when Wyatt came up to them. "Where *is* she?" His fists gripped Delacroix's shirt. "Did they hurt her?"

"She's injured." He carefully pulled Wyatt's hands away, trying to stay patient as he could understand what the other man was going through. "We should go see to her."

He led them to the parking lot to where he had left Lizzie. She made a frightful sight, her eyes closed, sweater bloody and ripped to shreds. Her breath ran ragged as she struggled to keep from sliding to the ground.

"Motherfucker!" Wyatt snarled as he pushed Delacroix and Mika aside to get to Lizzie. His face was red as he knelt down, but he didn't touch her, his arms remaining stiff at his sides. "I'm going to kill them!" he growled. "I swear to God, I'll rip every—"

"Wyatt, calm down," Mika said.

The normally unemotional Wyatt looked like he wanted to tear apart anything that moved. "Calm down? Look what they've done to her."

"We need to help her." Mika's voice was soothing. "Let's … you lift her up as gently as you can."

"Watch her back," Delacroix said as Wyatt gingerly slipped his arms under her. "She got clawed there."

Wyatt tucked Lizzie against his chest, her face buried in his shoulder as he lifted her up. She flinched, but then relaxed against him.

"I think she's already healing," Mika said. "But we should take her to HQ. Medical will patch her up."

As they all walked back to where the rest of the agents were, Delacroix leaned down to whisper in her ear, "I told you so."

His mate rolled her eyes.

———

With so many mage attacks happening in the last couple of months, the Guardian Initiative team had become efficient at concealing their activities. In less than thirty minutes, they cleaned up traces of the fight, gathered up and destroyed all CCTV footage in the area, and dosed witnesses with forgetting potion.

They gathered in the GI conference room for a debrief since they had a full house, with Daric joining them as he had just returned from another covert mission.

"Our 'guests' are now locked away safely in the basement level of the Fenrir Corp. headquarters," Arch began. "We'll contact the Lycan High Council in the morning and have them deal with those bastards. The Alpha will toss every charge he can at them, from breaking the Constanta Agreement, to hurting Lizzie."

"How is she?" Mika asked Wyatt.

"Resting," he answered stiffly. "Dr. Blake says she'll be fine by morning."

"Good." Mika turned to Delacroix. "Do you want to tell us why your former clan mates are after you?"

He stiffened in his chair, but Mika's comforting hand on his was like a soothing balm. This wasn't how he wanted her to find out about his past, but Lizzie had nearly died, and God knows what else could have happened to her, so he didn't have a choice. He only hoped Mika would be able to look him in the eye after he told his story.

"The Pont Saint-Louis clan took me in after I'd been abandoned by my parents," he began. "For the first few years, I was fostered with one of the older couples in the clan who didn't have their own children. But the wife died of a heart attack, and the husband didn't last for too long after that. I was just six years old." His memories of Marie and Albert Delacroix were fuzzy, though he knew he was never hungry or abused. "I bounced around from family to family, but when I turned ten and my powers showed up, Remy Boudreaux, the Alpha, took an interest in me."

Mika's face went pale. "What did he do?"

He swallowed the lump growing in his throat. "The Pont Saint-Louis was more gang than clan, and Remy was the big boss. Ruled his Lycans with an iron fist, and God save anyone who didn't follow his orders." Robbery, carjacking, loan-sharking, drugs, human trafficking, running guns—there was nothing he wouldn't do for money, and with a small army of Lycans at his side, he could do whatever he wanted. "When he found out what I could do, he put me to work right away."

"But you were a child," Arch said. "How could he?"

"He's pure evil," Cliff added.

"I had no choice." At least, he thought he didn't. "Remy used my powers for his own gain. At first, he would tell me to get into places and unlock the door so his guys could get in and rob the place. Then he asked me to start stealing things or leave messages for his enemies. If I didn't, I'd get beaten black and blue. Eventually, I got tired of being bloody and bruised all the time, so I just obeyed him. Started telling myself I wasn't hurtin' no one. At least not until ..."

His chest tightened; the air stuck in his lungs. But he had to say it. He looked at Mika, into the green depths of her eyes and prayed to God she could forgive him. "One night, he had me break into this house out in Lafayette. He normally didn't come out during these 'excursions,' but he wanted to be there for this one. That night it was just me an' him. We pull up to this big ol' house in the suburbs, one of them mansions with a large gate and security system. It was easy for me to slip inside and let him in. We go upstairs to the master bedroom where this couple was sleeping. I thought we would just scare them, but he takes out a gun and shoots them both."

Mika gasped, her hand tightening around his.

"I was shocked, I couldn't move. Remy starts ranting about how this guy swindled him out of money. One of those investment scams or some shit, I don't even remember what it was. We were leavin' when we hear this cry down the hallway."

The room was still and silent, the tension thick enough to cut with a knife. "We walk over and there was this nursery. The baby was wailin', and Remy hands me the gun and tells me to take care of it while he waited in the car." He closed his eyes, not wanting to see Mika's face. "I walked up to this infant and I pointed the gun, but I couldn't do it." The anguish at what he'd nearly done ate at him. "I'd already killed her parents—"

"You didn't, Marc." His eyes flew open and he could see the fury and determination on her face. "Remy pulled the trigger, not you."

"But if it wasn't for me, he wouldn't have gotten in."

"What happened?" Jacob asked.

"I took the baby and ran," he said. "Took it as far away as I could. Ended up in the next parish." It was the farthest he'd ever traveled in the shadows. "I left it at the nearest hospital, then I called Nick Vrost to get me out of there."

"The favor," Mika finished. "For saving Xavier's life."

He nodded. "But I had to get to New York first. I hitchhiked east with nothin' but the clothes on my back, eating food from dumpsters. I was just outside New Jersey when I found a way to call Vrost, and he picked me up."

"So, Remy wants you back?" Wyatt asked.

"Or dead?" Jacob added.

"They sent the shooter that night, but today, Alphonse said I would be coming with them," Delacroix said.

"It doesn't make sense," Mika said. "Why try to kill you and then nab you later?"

"Perhaps they changed their minds," Daric offered. "It's obvious they've been watching you, Delacroix. They knew to follow you to the carnival and take Lizzie to make you obey."

"What do we do now?" Cliff asked.

"We'll report them to the Lycan High Council," Wyatt said, his nostrils flaring. "They'll mete out the proper punishment for the Lycans that hurt Lizzie, and then Remy will have to submit to their investigation."

"That will have to wait until morning." Mika stood up. "For now, let's all go home and rest up. Marc?" Her eyes narrowed at him. "Everything all right?"

"It's fine, *cher*," he said. "Everything's fine."

But he knew it wasn't fine. Remy was after him for some reason, and he knew his former Alpha wasn't going to stop until he had what he wanted. The Lycan High Council had never stopped him before, and it wasn't going to now. He would send his people after him, as many as it took to take Delacroix in.

If he only had himself to worry about, then it wouldn't have mattered, but now he had Mika to think about, and if he hadn't yet, Remy would eventually figure out who she was to him. She couldn't be killed, but there were worst things than death, especially for females as he'd seen with Lizzie tonight. No, he couldn't let anything bad happen to her; he'd die first.

She's going to hate me, he thought, as a plan formed in his head. But he could apologize later. If he managed to get back to her alive.

CHAPTER FIFTEEN

Mika knew the moment her eyes opened that something was wrong. It was still dark, but her entire body was fully alert. Her wolf, it seemed, had woken her up, urging her to get out of bed. The space beside her was empty, but Delacroix's scent still lingered there, faint, as if he'd been up for a while. When her ears picked up the sound of the front doorknob turning, she got up as quick as her body would allow and dashed out to the living room.

"You're leaving."

Delacroix's body froze as he stood by the door, which was already halfway open. "It's not what you think, *cher*."

"Oh, yeah?" She marched over to him and poked his back with her finger. "You're all dressed up, you have a bag packed, and it's the middle of the fucking night!" Grabbing his shoulder, she forced him to face her. "So, tell me what the *hell* I'm thinking."

"I have to go."

"Go where? And without telling me?"

"I was going to call you ..."

"When? When you were halfway to Louisiana?" The look in his eyes told her she guessed his destination right.

He raked his palm down his face. "Mika, you don't know Remy. The council won't stop him. Nothing will, not until he gets what he wants."

"And so, you're going to serve yourself up to him? Just like that?" Her voice shook with anger. "Why the fuck would you do that?"

"Because I can't let him get to you!" His hands gripped her upper arms. "You don't know what he'll do. He didn't even care about that child. He would have had me kill an innocent baby ... who knows what he'll do to you when he finds out what you are to me?"

"What am I to you?" she spat back. "Because I don't feel like I matter at all, not if you're sneaking out in the middle of night, abandoning me—"

"*Mon Dieu*, Mika, I can't let anything happen to you. I love you too Goddamn much. I'm not as strong as you. If I lose you and the pup ..." He choked. "I wouldn't be able to go on."

"Marc." Oh God, he loved her. And she ... "Marc, nothing will happen to me, you know that." She reached up to cup her cheek. "I won't die, not while I'm carrying this baby."

"And what about after? You're only invulnerable while you're pregnant. And there are other things he can do to you ..."

He was right, of course. And though she really wanted to rip him a new one, she had to put herself in his position. "Marc, I understand why you think you had to run away, but Goddammit, this isn't just about you. We're mates. True

Mates, and we do things together now. Your problems are my problems, and if anyone tries to hurt you or our pup, I'm going to fucking murder them."

His dark eyes stared at her. "I can't let you—"

"Shut up and let me finish, Delacroix. I'm about to make a declaration of love here." A spark flashed in his eyes, and she couldn't help the smile curling up the sides of her lips. "I love you, okay?" She cupped his face in her hands. "Now, take your head outta your ass and sit down with me. We can solve this. You and me."

He looked stunned. "You love me?"

"Are you stupid, Delacroix? Of course I do. I—"

He kissed her urgently, his lips smothering hers, conquering and taking, but also in a way, it felt like a surrender. When he was done, he pressed his forehead to hers. "I love you."

"Then promise me you won't try to leave me again."

"I promise. There's nothin' in the world that could tear me away from you or our pup."

"Good. Now, tell me what you were trying to do."

He dropped his duffel bag to the floor and led her to the couch. "I wanted to make sure Remy never came after me or you ever again."

"How?"

"I was going to sneak back into Pont Saint-Louis and put a bullet in his head."

Just like Remy did with the baby's parents. "Surely it's not going to be that easy."

"It won't," he said. "Remy almost never sleeps, and he's always got someone guarding him. Also, by tomorrow morning, he'll know Alphonse and the others failed in their mission tonight. He would have had them checking in every hour. Most people underestimated Remy. Think that he's just another backwater redneck. But he's smart and a psychopath."

A deadly combination. "He knows you're coming."

"I bet he'll have his entire place lit up. No shadows. He made me tell him exactly how my powers worked, and I've taken him into the shadows myself."

"And you would have just walked in there?" Her blood pressure rose. "That is the stupidest thing I've ever heard."

"Never said I was smart, *cher.*"

"Fuck." She thought for a moment. They needed to take Remy out of the picture, without getting themselves killed. "I have an idea. And it doesn't involve killing him or getting yourself killed."

"*Cher*, there's no other way."

"You can't just walk in there and kill him. That's murder. The council will demand *your* head, and I won't be able to protect you." In the distant past, Lycans would settle things by killing and taking revenge on each other, but that only made it harder to keep their secret from the humans. The Lycan High Council was formed to keep peace and arbitrate disputes, as well as mete out appropriate punishments for Lycans who committed crimes or risked exposure to humans.

"Then what do you propose we do?"

"We need to gather evidence against him. Hit him where he'll hurt, which means taking down all his 'businesses.' He'll have his home secured at night, but what about other places? Does he have an office or a stash house?"

His brows knitted together. "I know a couple places."

"Good. We'll gather evidence and take it to high council.

We can even offer to take Remy in ourselves. With solid proof, they won't have a choice except to remove him as Alpha and send him away to the Lycan Siberian prison. Or worse." If they could find hard evidence that he really did kill those humans or anyone else, the council could order Remy be put down.

"I suppose that's a good plan, but I won't let you—"

"Won't let me what?" she challenged. "I told you, we're in this together. And the only way you'll stop me is if you lock me up. C'mon." She placed her hands on his shoulders. "You know this is an excellent plan. And there'll be no more bloodshed. No more violence."

He let out a long sigh. "All right, *cher*, we'll try it your way." His eyes took on a hard glint as his hands moved protectively over her belly. "But the moment you're in danger, I can't guarantee there won't be any bloodshed."

———

Mika was determined to see this through to the end. It was the only way she and Delacroix would ever have peace. When she told the rest of the team at GI what was happening, they all offered to help, but she wouldn't let them.

"We're already stretched thin as it is," she told them. "And this is a personal matter. If things go wrong, I can't have any of this blowing back on you or the clan." She had also informed Lucas of what she was planning, and he gave her his blessing.

"You'll need backup," Arch said. "What if he catches you?"

"Daric and Cross are in Moscow doing an important job,

so I can't just pull them out of that operation. But I've spoken to Daric, and I told him I would only call him if we needed him to transport us out and back here." Everyone in GI had a special token that was magically enhanced so either Daric or Cross could get to them in an emergency.

And so, Mika and Delacroix found themselves in Louisiana that same evening. Lucas had lent them his private plane, and they landed at an airstrip about thirty miles from Pont Saint-Louis. They rented a car and were soon headed toward the clan's territory.

"Remy's got a warehouse deep in the bayou," Delacroix said as they sped down the highway. "It's his biggest stash too. Drugs, guns, and God knows what else."

"We'll take photos and some evidence with us." She adjusted the button on her jacket where there was a hidden camera. "If we see a laptop or hard drives, we should take those too. How are we getting in?"

"We can't take the road into the warehouse," he said. "Remy'll have security around it. There's another way, but ... it's not safe."

"Not safe? How?"

"You'll see soon, *cher*."

They pulled off the freeway and onto a smaller highway. As they drove on, there were fewer and fewer houses dotting the countryside. Then they turned off onto a dirt road, drove for a few more minutes, before he stopped the car and killed the engine.

"We're here."

She got out of car. "Where are we?"

"The bayou, *cher*."

As her eyes adjusted to the dark, she realized they were

surrounded by thick vegetation and trees as tall as buildings. Their branches stretched out overhead, creating a natural canopy. The air was thick and musty, and the only sounds she could hear were the various critters scuttling around them. "Wow." She'd never seen anything like this.

"It's beautiful, yes, but like I said, dangerous. We gotta be careful of the gators."

"There're alligators in there?" she asked incredulously.

"*Oui*, but they don't bother us as long as we don't bother them. Now, let's go." He gestured toward the boat tied up at the end of a short dock that jutted out into the water. "I'll have to paddle us up. They'll hear any engine approaching."

He led her to the boat and helped her inside. It was difficult to find a comfortable position, especially in her condition, but she managed to tuck her legs under her as she sat on the middle seat. She felt the little dinghy sway and dip as he positioned himself behind her and took up the paddles.

"We'll come around the back of the property, say, a good fifty feet from the warehouse. I'll find a suitable place where we can travel through the shadows and get us inside without anyone knowing. Remy'll have at least two guys there, plus a whole load of cameras and motion sensors."

"Hopefully we can get in and out quickly." A knot in her stomach formed, and she wondered if this was going to work. *It has to.* This was the only way to get Remy out of the picture. "How much further?" They seemed to have gone deeper into the bayou, as her enhanced hearing couldn't even pick up any signs of civilization. Just insects, small animals, and the *whoosh* of the boat as it sliced through the water. And, thankfully, no slithering gators.

"It's much farther than I thought," he said. "I've never

taken this way, Remy never let me. Forbade me to come near the swamps." He shuddered. "I don't even know how to swim."

"You don't swim?" She jerked her head back at him. "Seriously?"

"*Oui.*"

"What if we capsize? Or the boat springs a leak? Or—"

"Shh ... don't worry your pretty little head, *cher.*" He flashed her a grin. "I'll—" The smile faded from his lips.

"Marc?" Her neck was getting strained, so she turned around carefully. "What's wrong? You look like you've seen a ghost."

His mouth parted. "Do you hear that?"

She looked around them. "Hear what?"

"Somethin's calling me." He blinked. "I have to—" He stopped as the boat jerked.

"Marc!" she screamed and grabbed onto him. The boat began to move sideward, like a force was pulling them to shore. His arms tightened around her as they moved faster, the side of the boat hitting land so hard, they tumbled out. Immediately, he shielded her, wrapping his body around so she landed on him, instead of the ground.

"Oomph!" She braced herself against him. "What the hell?"

He quickly hauled her up to her feet, then her vision went dark as he pulled them back into the shadows. "Stay still, *cher*. I don't know what—"

Air rushed out of her lungs as she felt her body being pushed forward, and she fell, landing on her hands and knees. She ignored the pain that shot up her limbs as she struggled for breath. Looking around her, she realized her vision had gone back to normal. "What happened?"

He was on his knees too, his hands braced on the ground, shaking his head. "I ... I don't know. It was like someone reached in and kicked me out of the shadows."

"Who are you and how'd you do that?"

Mika froze when she felt the presence in front of them. The person—female, from the voice—didn't smell like a Lycan or a human for that matter. Witch, then. Slowly, she lifted her head.

Staring down at her was an older woman, probably in her late forties to early fifties, with light brown hair that came to her waist. The expression on her face was stern, and Mika felt the power she radiated as those dark eyes seemed to bore into her.

Beside her was a girl, maybe thirteen or fourteen. She looked like a younger version of the woman. The expression on her face was curious, and her ebony eyes darted from Mika to Delacroix.

"I said, who are you and how did you *do* that?" The woman repeated, a ripple of energy pulsed all around them.

Her wolf immediately went into defense mode, raising its hackles and baring its teeth.

Delacroix reached over to wrap a hand around her arm. "She's ... using the energy of the shadows ... I don't know how but—"

"Lycans," the woman spat. "Didn't we tell your Alpha to never cross into our territory again?"

"We're not from Boudreaux's clan," she said, trying to keep her wolf leashed. It was a difficult task, seeing as her animal was extra protective because of their pup.

"Then what you creepin' 'round here for? And"—her eyes blazed at Delacroix—"how are you able to walk the dark trail?"

"Walk the dark trail?" he asked.

"You moved into the shadows," she said, her teeth gritting together. "You can access dark magic. But you're a Lycan. How could that be?"

"Mama." The young girl grabbed the woman's hand and tugged excitedly. "He's like us." She smiled shyly at them. "I see the magic surrounding him. Like yours." She waved her hand around her mother's shape. "And mine."

The woman's brows snapped together. "Marina ... are you sure?"

"Yes, Mama." She squinted at Mika. "And you! You're glowing."

What did the girl mean? "Glowing?"

"Come," the woman said before Mika could ask further. "Get up. We're gonna figure this out now."

Mika and Delacroix looked at each other. "Not like we have a choice," she said.

"No." His mouth pulled back into a hard line. "And I have this feeling ... I need to know."

She wished she could read his mind, because so many emotions flashed on his face in such a short span. "Let's go then."

Delacroix got up first, and then helped her up. When the woman saw Mika's pregnant belly, she muttered a string of curses. "I wouldn't have ... if I had known."

"I'm fine." She dusted the dirt off her jeans. There was a feeling of relief that swept over her at the other woman's concern. It at least reassured her that they wouldn't hurt her or her baby.

They followed the woman and her daughter deeper into the woods, walking through the dense and thick plant life. Though there was no trail, they both seemed to know where to go. Mika saw a light up ahead, which she guessed was their destination. A few seconds later, they emerged into a clearing.

The air here seemed different, why, she didn't know. Seven cabins stood in a semi-circle in the middle of the clearing, and they were led toward the one in the middle. There was a light coming from inside, and thick smoke curled up from the chimney.

"Stay here," the woman instructed as she walked up the porch steps. She was about to open the door when it flew open, and another figure trudged out. "Mama?"

"Gabrielle! What's goin' on? Did you feel it?" came the deep, gravelly voice. "Somethin' disturbs the shadows. I—" She hobbled forward with a careful gait, the light slowly revealing long locks of white hair framing a wrinkled face, and dark eyes that were as sharp as blades.

"He can walk the dark trail, Mama," the woman said.

"Come closer, boy," the crone said, gesturing with her withered fingers.

Delacroix took a step forward, his face expressionless. "I've lived in Pont Saint-Louis all my life. Never knew there were witches around these parts."

Her mouth opened as she gasped. "You ..."

The woman—Gabrielle—moved protectively in front of the old woman. "Mama, what's wrong? Do you know this man?"

Those obsidian eyes never left Delacroix. "You're alive."

His brows knit in confusion. "Last I checked."

"You were lost ... we were told you had died, but ... you're here. Child of the shadows, you are *home*." Tears glistened on the woman's weathered cheeks, and she lunged forward, seemingly finding a surge of youthful energy. She nearly toppled down the stairs, and Delacroix caught her in an instant, arms going around her before she fell.

There was a crackle of energy there—recognition—as the two came face-to-face.

"Mama, what's going on?" Gabrielle asked as she rushed toward them. "Take your hands away from my—"

"Gabrielle, oh, Gabrielle, don't you see? I know you don't have the sight, but *look*." The woman sobbed. "Look into his eyes. Eyes passed down from our ancestors. Beaumont eyes."

Mika did a double take. It had been staring her in the face the whole time, yet her brain didn't put it together. Delacroix. Gabrielle. Marina. And the old woman. They all had the same eyes. "Are you—"

"You're him. Who else could you be? She could walk the dark trail too." The old woman pressed her face to his cheek. "You're my Helene's baby."

"H-Helene?" he stuttered.

"My daughter. You're Helene Beaumont's son. And my grandson."

"I ... it can't ..."

"Of course you are," the old woman insisted. "She was your father's True Mate. When she found out about you, she was so happy. And so was your father ..." A whimper escaped her mouth.

"My ... mother and father? But I was told I was abandoned." His face went pale. "I don't understand."

The old woman took a deep breath. "Come, child, follow your *mémère*. Let's go inside. I have some *étouffée* on the stove. It'll warm your stomach and cure what ails you. Bring your True Mate along." She winked at Mika, turned around, and headed inside, Gabrielle and Marina at her heels.

Mika's jaw dropped. *How did the old woman know?*

Delacroix took her hand in his. "I don't know if I can do this."

"You can." She squeezed his hand. "I'll be here. I won't leave."

With a decisive nod, he led her up the porch steps.

CHAPTER SIXTEEN

THE SMELL OF SPICES, SAVORY TOMATOES, AND CRAWFISH
tickled Delacroix's nose as they entered the old woman's—his
grandmother's, apparently—house. It wasn't grand or fancy,
but it was clean, the wood floors scrubbed down, the couch
overstuffed and comfy, and various knickknacks displayed all
over. If he ever dreamed of what a home would be like while
growing up, he supposed this is what it would have been.

"Come see, come see." She gestured to the table with her
gnarled hands. "Sit, both of you."

He itched for her to move faster, but from the look
Gabrielle had given him, he knew it was best to let the old
woman go at her pace. He pulled out a chair for Mika and
then sat beside her at the large kitchen table. Much like the
rest of the furniture, it was well-used and serviceable, and he
could imagine hundreds of family meals eaten here. Meals
his mother had eaten.

The revelation of his mother's family had been a shock,
one that he hadn't quite recovered from. So many questions
loomed in his mind all at once. Growing up, he'd been

reminded by Remy over and over again that his parents abandoned him, so he never cared much for them. They didn't want him, and so he didn't want them either. Now ...

The sound of bowls clattering on the wooden table knocked him out of his thoughts.

"Eat," the old woman urged. "It's good, good, eh?"

He picked up a spoon and took a bite of the hot stew. "Delicious," he said politely. It probably was, but he couldn't concentrate on the taste.

Beside him, Mika took a spoonful in her mouth. "Oh, wow. That's like, the best thing I've ever tasted." She ate a few more spoonfuls. "Oh God, that really did cure what ails me."

The old woman laughed. "I like her, your mate."

Mika swallowed the mouthful she had in her mouth. "Um, I was wondering, ma'am, how did you know?"

"That you are my grandson's mate?" She looked at Mika's stomach. "I suppose anyone could have guessed, but I have the sight, you know."

"The sight?" she echoed. "As in, you can see the future?"

She clucked her tongue and eased herself onto a chair, Gabrielle assisting her. "Forgive me, I haven't introduced myself. My name is Adelaide. Adelaide Beaumont. And this is my daughter, Gabrielle, and my granddaughter, Marina."

"I'm Mika Westbrooke. And this is, er, Marc Delacroix."

"Good, strong name. Taken from the god of war." A warm smile touched her lips as she fixed her gaze on him, her expression wistful. "My elder daughter, Helene, was just like you. She too, had the power to go into the shadows. 'Walk the dark trail' as we call it. One day, about thirty-five years ago, she came to me and said she met someone special and wanted me to meet him. He came here to this house, and I knew it. I saw it."

"Saw what?" he asked.

"My powers—the dark sight, we call it. No, it does not show me the future. It shows me magic. I can sense power in others, as well as residual power when someone touches an object with great magic. But what I saw with them ... it was the most beautiful thing I'd ever seen." Her eyes shone with tears. "It looked like a golden thread, so delicate and shiny, linking him to Helene. They both shone like two bright stars who only orbited around each other."

"I can see it too, *Mémère*," Marina chirped and pointed to Mika and Delacroix. "I can see the dark glow around him, like you and Mama. But her ... it's magic, but different." She gestured to the empty space between them. "And the string ..."

Adelaide smiled warmly at the girl. "*Oui, ma chevrette.*"

"You could see their True Mate bond?" Mika's eyes went wide.

"I can, just as I can see yours and my grandson's. And it's beautiful and pulses with life when you're carrying. That's how I knew Helene was pregnant with you," she said to Delacroix. "She was so happy when I told her."

"Then why did they abandon me?" Marc asked, his voice tight.

Adelaide pressed a hand to her chest. "Is that what you were told? Then you were lied to. We all were." Her hand shook as she placed it over his. "He told us you died. I never believed it."

The lump forming in his throat made it hard to breathe or speak.

"Who did?" Mika asked when he didn't say anything.

"Remy Boudreaux, your father's Alpha. He didn't approve of the match. Hated what she was," she said, gnashing her teeth. "But he allowed them to live on their territory, but forbade us to come visit. One day, he sent over one of his lackeys. Told us that Helene died in childbirth. Sent her ashes back to us. Hers and the child's, they said, because you were stillborn." She sobbed hard, and Gabrielle placed an arm around her as Marina wrapped her arms around her waist.

"And my father?" he managed to croak out.

"He said he was killed by a gang of Lone Wolves when they broke into their home. That's what made her go into labor early and die."

The information was still processing in his head. "What was my father's name?" he asked.

"Armand Delacroix."

"Delacroix?"

"Yes," Adelaide said. "What's wrong?"

"I was fostered with a couple named Delacroix, but they died a few years after they took me in. No one told me if I was related to them. Were they my grandparents?"

"I'm not sure, child." She reached over and squeezed his hand. "I don't even know why Boudreaux would lie to all of us."

"Isn't it obvious?" Gabrielle said bitterly. "Remy killed them. I know it."

"How are you sure?" Mika asked.

"Armand loved her so much, and once the baby—Marc— was born, they were planning to leave the clan. He would go Lone Wolf and live here with us. Remy must have found out and killed them. Helene told me ..." She took a deep breath. "Remy acted strange around her ... she thinks while Remy hated what she was, he also wanted her for himself. I think he was in love with her."

It was all starting to make sense. Why Remy hated him too, but yet kept him around. Why he arranged for him to be fostered with his family, but didn't tell anyone who he really was.

"All this time ... I knew in my heart there was something wrong with the story. My poor Helene," Adelaide wailed.

"I'm so sorry," Mika said. "And I hope you know, not all our kind hates witches. In fact, we have several witches and warlocks who found their True Mates with our clans. Their children are like your grandson—hybrids, we call them."

"We know about them," Gabrielle offered. "But do not lump us together with all witches."

"Wait, you mean, you're not witches?" Mika frowned. "But you have magic."

"We do," Gabrielle said. "But we are not like your nature witches. They call us swamp witches, at least they did when we still associated with them." Her nose wrinkled. "We use dark magic, very different from their light magic."

"Do not be afraid," Adelaide said when Mika let out a horrified gasp. "Dark magic is not evil. It's not bad, just another facet of magic. Even the moon must have a dark and light side, one bathed in nature's light and the other in its shadow."

"But what about blood magic?" Mika said.

Gabrielle recoiled. "Blood magic? How does a Lycan know of such things?"

"Our enemies use it." She quickly told them about the mages, at least the short version.

"Bad *gris-gris*, blood magic," Adelaide said with a tsk. "We stay away from it. For decades, my family and I have kept to ourselves, because we do not like to get involved in wars."

"It has kept us safe. Kept our children safe," Gabrielle said as she patted Marina's head. "Our dark magic keeps most people away from us. Surrounds our home so no one can harm us."

"I can't explain it, but I heard it calling to me." Just like the first time he had heard the shadow call him. "And then we were pulled to shore."

"I felt him too," Gabrielle said. "At first, I thought that someone had penetrated our shields. I was the one that hauled your boat to shore."

"You can control shadows," he deduced. "That's how you kicked me out."

She nodded. "Helene and I used to play this game. She would hide in the shadows and I would try to find her, and when I did, I would push her out."

"It's fate that you came to us, Marc," Adelaide said.

"Oh, shit!" Mika blurted out. "Sorry ... this really is amazing, but that's not quite the reason we came here."

He nearly forgot about Remy. But when he remembered that bastard, rage pumped through his veins. "We're here for Remy. We have to make him pay."

"Marc," Mika said. "I know you're furious at him—hell, that probably doesn't even begin to describe how you're feeling. But we can't kill him. You know that. If the Council finds out—"

"You're here for Remy Boudreaux?" Gabrielle got up from her chair, the legs scraping across the wooden floor. "I want to go with you."

"We have to take him in alive," Mika said. "We have a council that governs us, and if they find out we killed him, they'll come down on Marc and I."

"But we're not part of any council." Adelaide's eyes burned with the fire of someone decades younger. "We will avenge my Helene."

"And my father," he said. "Mika ... your plan was brilliant. But you know this is what has to happen. You have no idea what Remy is like. You're a leader, too, and you have to make hard decisions sometimes. Remy wouldn't hesitate to kill you or any of us."

"I—" She took a deep breath. "We need a confession from him. We have to be sure it was him."

"Oh, he will confess," Gabrielle clasped her hands together. "I will make sure of it."

"We strike tonight." Adelaide stood, her eyes still ablaze. "He will not expect it."

"Tonight?" Mika said. "But Remy has a lot of wolves. There's only us."

"We are not alone." Gabrielle smiled. "The entire Beaumont clan will join us. To avenge our Helene. And Marc, who's been kept from us all these years."

"Marc," Adelaide turned her gaze to him. "It's time for you to meet the rest of the family."

CHAPTER SEVENTEEN

THE BOATS MOVED THROUGH THE WATER, SILENT AS shadows, floating along the bayou towards one destination.

He should feel some fear, seeing as they were about to take on his former clan, but Delacroix was calm. This feeling, he couldn't describe it except that it was like he belonged, not just to this place, but to these people.

About twenty or so were with them now, all piled into the half a dozen boats floating along the bayou. Even now, with what lay ahead, there was that sense that this was where he was supposed to be, with his people. There were seven families who lived in the swamps, nearly fifty people in total. His introduction to them had been brief, and he didn't have time to learn all their names, but they all immediately welcomed him without hesitation. And when they learned of Remy's betrayal, each one was eager to join them.

"All of you have blessed powers?" Mika had asked. Most witches only had the power to cast spells and potions, and the few who had active powers, like Jacob or Lizzie, were called blessed witches.

"Most of us do in some shape or form," Gabrielle replied. "And we have a stockpile of potions we can use to confuse and stun our enemies. Not a lot, because they cost a lot to make, but there is no better time than now to use them."

"We'll definitely be a more even match then," he had said, and with all the pieces in place, they began to plan and strategize how they were going to get to Remy.

The first part of their plan was to sneak up on them by way of the swamps, not to the warehouse but his actual home where Remy would be holed up and surrounded by most of his Lycans. He realized now the reason Remy told them to never go near the water, and him in particular. He was afraid Delacroix might discover his real identity if he ever got too close to the Beaumont's territory.

Remy's house was another couple of miles down the bayou, and it took them a while longer to get there seeing as they had to use the shadows to propel them. Gabrielle and another witch with similar powers used the darkness to push the boats in a slow, silent procession, and they all knew to keep noise to a minimum.

Beside him, Mika slipped her hand into his and gave him a squeeze. He knew he couldn't ask her to sit this out, as she was determined to see this through. However, she agreed to stay in the rear and protect Adelaide, who had insisted on coming as she demanded to be able to look Remy in the eye when he finally confessed the truth.

A short whistle rang out, catching everyone's attention. He focused his gaze up ahead. *Just as I thought.* Remy's property was lit up like Rockefeller Center at Christmas. Flood lights surrounded the property. Remy knew that for him to travel from shadow to shadow, he would have to see his destination, and with no shadow anywhere, Delacroix wouldn't be able to get near the house unless he walked right up to the front door.

Gabrielle let out a low whistle, the signal to get ready. She raised her hands, and the boats slowed to a stop as they approached the shore. One by one, they hopped over the side and waded through the waist-deep water, the shadows concealing any noise they made.

He glanced around. No one seemed nervous or worried, and so he decided he would assume they could all handle themselves.

When they were all assembled on the shore, Gabrielle signaled for one of her cousins, Aurelie, to come up front. "Now," she whispered, and the other witch nodded. She closed her eyes and took a deep breath.

Slowly, a dark fog enveloped her, then flattened to the ground. The shadow began to spread farther, in the direction of the house. "Rising darkness," Gabrielle had called it. The ability to create shadows.

"It's time," Gabrielle said.

He looked at Mika, then gave her a brief kiss on the lips. "I'll see you soon, *cher*."

Her green eyes glowed in the dark. "See you soon."

After a quick nod to Gabrielle, he walked toward the shadow Aurelie created and walked into it. It was a narrow strip, as Aurelie could only produce a limited amount, but it was long enough for him to reach one of the generators that powered the freestanding flood lights illuminating the property. Once he got near it, he shut it off, and the area plunged into darkness.

He heard a commotion from inside the house, and a few

seconds later, the door opened. A man came strolling out, one of Remy's lackeys, and headed toward the generators. Delacroix sprang into action as soon as the man was close enough, grabbing him and taking him into the darkness.

"*Merde!* Where the fuck—Help!" He screamed as he tried to get away, but Delacroix threw a small bottle of knock out potion at him, and he crumpled to the ground. Once he was sure the other man was completely out cold, he dragged him as far away from the house as possible and tied and gagged him.

A few minutes later, another Lycan came out of the house. Delacroix repeated his earlier actions, dumping the unconscious man next to his companion.

He waited in the darkness, the seconds ticking by as he watched the front door. There was noise coming from inside the house, this time, hushed whispers. His instinct told him that they knew something was up. Remy wasn't stupid, after all.

The front door opened, and paws pounded on the front porch as several Lycans poured out onto the front lawn, already in wolf form. Lycans were much larger than their animal counterparts, and even one that wasn't well-trained in combat could do a lot of damage, and Remy made sure all his wolves knew how to fight.

That was why the Beaumonts would have to use every advantage they could. They stayed in the shadows, waiting for their enemies to advance. The Lycans would be able to see them in the dark, but that was the idea. Their one advantage wasn't that they could stay hidden, but the *shadows* themselves. Everyone scattered about, and so the Lycans spread out. Just as planned.

A long, high-pitched whistle rang out, followed by two short bursts. That was the signal. Delacroix began to shift into his wolf form as the witches and warlocks held their positions.

He charged forward, moving into the shadows before reappearing behind two wolves in the back of the line. The element of surprise was on his side, so they didn't notice him until it was too late. He sank his teeth into the neck of the larger one, digging deep until blood flooded his mouth, then did the same with the other. Though it might be inevitable, he wanted to avoid having to kill his kind, so he tried his best not to make it a fatal wound, but only slow down his opponents.

As the other wolf staggered to the ground, whining in pain, Delacroix's wolf glanced around, using his enhanced vision. The Beaumonts were definitely holding their own, and the display of powers was impressive to say the least. One witch created a shield made of shadows, which stopped two wolves from knocking her down. Another seemed to be forming a dark fog over the eyes of a large gray wolf, blinding it. One of the older warlocks was surrounded by three wolves, and Delacroix was ready to charge in and help him when he turned into a dark gas and dissipated, only to re-form outside the circle, then hit them with a bottle of potion that knocked them out.

Knowing his relatives would be able to take care of their enemies, he shifted back into his human form and stalked up to the main house. His heart thumped so loudly in his chest, it was the only thing he could hear.

He was afraid of Remy; he had no problem admitting it. The man abused and tortured him, physically and mentally, making him feel worthless and unable to escape. It wasn't until he saw that innocent child, and faced with the horrific thing he'd done, that he found the courage to run away.

And now, it could be his very own child's future at stake. Remy would get his revenge at any cost. His mate and pup would never be safe until he was gone from this world. Delacroix wasn't sure if he would be able to wait for a confession; even if Remy didn't kill Helene and Armand, he already knew the Alpha was guilty of other things that he should answer for. If the Lycan High Council decided he should die for killing Remy, then he would be able to go gladly, knowing his family was safe.

With a determined stride, he drew closer to the house, ready to charge up the porch steps when the door flew open.

"What the fuck is—you!" Blue eyes blazed with anger. "*Feet pue tan*! I should have known." Remy Boudreaux's reputation preceded him, and he was known to many as a cruel and heartless bastard. Many perhaps pictured him as a cartoon villain or typical Hollywood bad guy, but many who met him for the first time were immediately arrested by his good looks. He was over six feet tall, extremely fit for a man who was nearly sixty years old, and had the face of an angel— a blond, blue-eyed Lucifer who seemed ageless. It was the hard, cruel glint in his eyes that gave away the ugliness in his soul.

"Remy," he said. "You know why I'm here."

"Seems like you just made things easier for me," the Alpha replied smugly. "I should thank you for that, Delacroix. Saved me the trouble of havin' to collect you myself."

"So, were you trying to kill me or get me back? Still sore that you couldn't order me around anymore?"

Remy barked out a laugh. "You must have thought you were so smart, getting that transfer right under my nose." He spat on the ground.

"You should have left me alone, Remy. You have more than enough wolves to do your dirty work."

His mouth curled up in arrogance. "You think I needed you and your powers? Ha! I didn't need you. But your little disappearin' act started a little rebellion among the younger ones." Remy started training his wolves young. Training them to fear him, anyway. "Thought they could get out too. But I had to show them that wasn't an option, and if they left, there was nowhere on earth they could hide from me."

"Well, your assassin wasn't successful."

"And he paid for it with his life." His nostrils flared. "But then again, I got a better offer."

"Offer?"

"Seems your new clan has made enemies. Powerful enemies. That red-eyed, bald headed *diable* wanted to get his hands on you."

"Red-eyed devil ..." Then it struck him, who Remy was referring to. He'd seen them before, back in that cell in Zhobghadi. "You made a bargain with the *mages*? Don't you know what they want?"

"They were willing to pay a lot for you," Remy said. "Much more than I thought you'd be worth."

"You fool," he said. "The mages will kill you the first chance they get. Don't you know anythin'?"

"I'm a fool?" Remy shouted. "*Non.* You are the *coullion.* What about you? Comin' here to take me on by yourself?

Even if you did succeed in killing me, you'd never leave here alive."

Ah, now this was what he was waiting for. "Why don't you call your wolves then?"

"Gladly." He let out a series of whistles, a signal that Delacroix knew was meant to have everyone come back to gather around him. A few seconds passed and there was nothing. No sound of feet or paws coming back or howls to acknowledge they had heard his call. Remy repeated it, louder, but it was only greeted with silence. His jaw hardened, and eyes filled with hate turned to him. "What did you do?"

"I didn't come alone. I had help."

"Help?"

"Yes. From my mother's family. The Beaumonts."

Remy's face twisted in hate. "Those dirty bitches!" he screamed. "What did they do to my wolves?"

"You may hate magic, Remy, but it has its uses. Like a little somethin' they call 'shield of darkness.' It can block out any sound or light, even from Lycan senses." One of his witch cousins had snuck around the back and created the shield around the perimeter of the house and the yard, which was why they couldn't hear what was going on around them. "As we speak, the Beaumonts are taking down all your wolves."

"*Pic kee toi!*" Remy ran forward, launching himself off the porch and toward him as he began to shift. Delacroix stepped into the shadows so Remy's partially-shifted form landed on the ground. Re-emerging from behind, he pinned the Alpha down as he lay vulnerable in mid-shift.

"Give up, Remy!"

The Alpha let out a snarl and swiped a claw back at him,

barely missing his face. He pinned him harder to the ground, using his own bodyweight as leverage. He managed to hold on for a few seconds, but Remy somehow broke free of his grasp and scrambled to his feet.

"It's over, Remy," Delacroix said as he got up. "No one's coming to your rescue. We can fight it out if you want, but even if you killed me, the Beaumonts will come after you."

"I should have gotten rid of you when I had the chance!" Remy shouted. "Why I let you live after Helene died, I don't know!"

Rage was burning inside him for the mother he never knew, but he kept it reined in. "Did you kill her?"

"Kill Helene?" he roared. "I *loved* her." An angry snarl contorted his lips. "But my wolf hated her. Hated what she was. And hated me because I couldn't stay away."

Delacroix stared at him, stunned, as he could clearly see the anguish and conflict inside him. Wolf and man, sharing the same body but wanting different things. "Your wolf—"

There was a flash of pain there in his eyes. "We met Helene at the same time, your father and I, at the diner where she worked. But she only had eyes for Armand from the first moment. They said they were True Mates, and you were the proof. So, I allowed it, allowed her to live in our territory because I couldn't bear the thought of not seeing her. I kept fighting with my wolf; it wanted her gone. One night, I decided to show my animal it couldn't control me, so I went to her." His voice dropped to a whisper. "She was alone. Your father was working a double. And I told her I wanted her and loved her. She couldn't believe it and said I was mistaken. Demanded I leave but ... my wolf it was already lunging for her. And so, she ran. It went after her. She hid in the shadows for as long as she could, but my wolf searched for her the entire night. It was your cry that gave you away and I knew that she'd given birth to you."

Numbness overtook him and if he hadn't shaken his head to clear his thoughts, he surely would have sunk to his knees. Child of the shadows ... in more ways than one it seemed.

"My wolf tracked her down from the smell of her blood and your cries. And it ... when it saw the two of you ... they said she couldn't be harmed!" he cried. "She was supposed to be invulnerable. That's what they said."

"Only while she's pregnant!" he spat. "You didn't know, did you?"

He let out pained groan. "By the time I was able to wrestle back control from my wolf, she was ... she was ... gone." The agony in his voice was real. He really did believe he loved Helene. "And then your father was there. He must have realized that she had run and tracked her down. Saw she was dead. He came at me, but he was so blinded by grief that I easily took him down. Then I made up that story about a gang of Lone Wolves breaking into their home. But I had to hide you, so ... I went to Armand's great-uncle and aunt, told them to never reveal who you were because the Lone Wolves were still after you."

So that's who they were. Perhaps there was a small part of Remy—maybe the part that loved Helene—that was still good, which was why he didn't kill Delacroix when he was an infant. But that didn't mean he wasn't a murderer. "You killed my mother."

"It wasn't me! It was my wolf. I loved her and would never—"

"But *you* still killed my father!" His hands curled into

fists. He could end Remy right now. Drag him into the shadows, and no one would ever know. He should have done it a long time ago. "And the things you made me do ..."

"You didn't take care of that child in Lafayette, did you?" Remy taunted, reminding him of that night. "You spared her. So, I know you don't have the guts to kill me."

"Like I said, it's over, Remy." There had been so much blood and violence in his life, one would think one more death wouldn't have mattered. But this was not the kind of world he wanted his pup to grow up in. "We're taking you in. To the Lycan High Council, and you'll have to answer for your crimes."

"The council?" He sneered. "I'd rather die at your hands. Not that you'd ever have the chance."

Remy's hand shot out so quickly, he didn't have time to think about what to do. A bright light turned his vision into a blinding white screen. Before he could react, his back hit the ground, and a heavy weight pressed on top him.

"Like my little trick? You should thank the mages for that potion. Now, I'm gonna hurt you just enough to keep you alive until they—*arrggh!*"

The weight lifted off of him as Remy howled out in pain. He was still blinded, but as he struggled to get up, a pair of hands gripped his arm. The scent of lavender and spice tickled his nostrils.

"It's me," Mika whispered in an aching voice. "I thought he—"

"I'm fine, but ... I can't see. Must have been a blinding potion. What's happening?"

She let out a relieved breath. "Gabrielle ... she has Remy

subdued now. He's not getting away. Oh my God, I didn't realize she could control her powers that way."

Damn, he wished he could see it. "Help me up ..." She slung an arm under him and assisted him to his feet. The first thing he did was embrace her and bury his nose in her hair, then moved his hand to her belly. "Everything all right?"

"I'm fine, we both are." He felt her sigh against his chest. "And your grandmother is here too."

"Adelaide? Are you—"

"I'm fine, child. I heard everything; we all did."

Mika cleared her throat and moved out of his arms. "I need to make a phone call," she said. "I won't be too far away." He felt her squeeze his hand before her hand slipped away.

Long thin fingers wrapped over his hand. "Thank you," Adelaide whispered. "Because of you, we will finally be able to get justice for Helene and Armand."

His throat burned, so all he could do was nod. "I'm sorry I couldn't kill him. I just thought—"

"Shh. It's all right. I understand. It has to end, all this death and blood." Her voice was wistful, and he could picture a sad smile on her face. "My Helene ... she was the gentle one. Hated conflict of any kind ... the p-peacemaker of the family." Her voice grew shaky. "She would have been proud of you."

As he heard the old woman sob, he turned toward her direction, reaching out to her. His grandmother fell into his arms as her thin, frail frame shook with sobs and wails. He soothed her, whispering to her in French and English as he rubbed his hand down her back. They stood there for a long while, and by the time she slowed down, his vision had fully returned.

"Th-thank you," she hiccupped as she stepped away.

"You're welcome." Glancing around, he saw his aunt a few feet away from them standing over Remy. "Gabrielle? Is he—"

"I haven't killed him," she replied. "Yet."

The Alpha lay on the ground as strips of dark fog wrapped around his legs and arms, pinning him to the ground. The lower half of his face was also covered in a mask of shadow, preventing him from speaking or turning his head, but the fury in his eyes completely conveyed how he was feeling at the moment.

"How's everyone else?" he asked Mika as she came back. "Did they—"

"All the wolves have been subdued." She put her phone back into her coat pocket. "No casualties. I've also called Daric. He'll be here soon with reinforcements. We'll take everyone back to Fenrir."

He huffed out a breath. "Almost forgot to tell you something Remy said." He quickly relayed the story about how a mage came to the Alpha and struck his bargain.

"Sounds like they wanted to turn you into one of them," Mika said, huffing out a breath. "I'll tell Daric when he gets here. He'll be interested to know, I'm sure."

"What about your council?" Adelaide asked. "Will they give us justice? Without any consequences on my grandson or your clan?"

"The Alpha is calling the Lycan High Council as we speak," Mika said. "Lucas will relay the events to them, and

I'm sure once they realize what Remy did and what he was up to, they'll side with us."

"I wish my Helene was still alive," Adelaide said. "But we cannot change the past. And I'm glad you have come back to us." Her expression was full of hope as she looked up at him. "You will ... stay and get to know us, right? I mean, for a little while, before you have to go back to your clan?"

He slipped his hand into hers. "Of course. We are family ... *Mémère*."

The smile on the old lady's face could have lit up the night. "That we are." She turned to Mika and took her hand, all three of them linked. "And soon there will be more of us."

His heart nearly burst his chest with happiness. Growing up, he'd been alone; surrounded by his clan, yes, but always alone, with only the shadow as his companion. But now, he not only had a mate and a pup on the way, but a whole family he never knew about, and a legacy that he would hopefully be passing on to his children.

Shadow and light were facets of life and nature, one couldn't exist without the other. And though he was a child of the cold darkness, from now on, his life would always be filled with the warmth of light from the love surrounding him.

EPILOGUE

Mika took a deep breath, taking in as much of the fresh, clean air as she could into her lungs. "That winter felt like it was forever. I'm glad it's done. Don't you love spring?" she asked her mate. "Everything's so fresh and clean."

"Growin' up, I never really noticed the weather, *cher*." He helped her out of the car and shut the door behind her. "In the bayou, summers are long and hot. Everythin' else is just wet and cloudy."

"But surely you can appreciate this weather," she said. "Spring is always like a new beginning.

He stopped and placed a hand on her belly. "I never thought I could start again, but maybe now I believe it. You've given me a new life."

His smile made warmth spread through her. "New beginnings are always something to be happy about. But," she put her hand over his, "sometimes there's no reason to start again. Sometimes you're just fine the way you are."

He pressed his nose into her hair and inhaled. "Then you've given me something else. Something more precious than my own life."

Some days Mika couldn't believe this was her life now. A few months ago, she'd been consumed by her own depression, drowning herself in work, and at the same time, trying to fill that void inside her with something. She thought a pup would be able to do that, and while she knew that she would be devoted to that life growing inside her, she now had so much more. She had a mate, and soon they would be a family. She was happy and content, and it was obvious that Delacroix would be an excellent father. They both had their fears and doubts, but she knew that together, they would be able to raise this child and give it so much love.

"Are you sure you really want to do this?"

He nodded without hesitation. "I'm doing this for you and for me. I think ... I think it's time."

She slipped her hand into his and squeezed. "You know I love you now, right?"

"I do, Mika." And she had no doubt.

"Okay, let's go then."

Together, hand in hand, they walked through the gates of Holy Memorial Cemetery. When they reached Joe's grave, she placed her free hand on top of his gravestone.

"Hey, babe," she began. "Sorry I haven't been back for months. I've been really busy, but I'm here now. I wanted to say ..." Her throat tightened, and her chest ached. "I'm sorry. I can't," she said to Delacroix.

"It's all right, *cher*." He squeezed her hand tighter. "You probably feel like a part of you died when he did. That's all right. Maybe that part belongs to him, and I would never ask you to take it back."

Her breath hitched, but the ache in her chest loosened. She knew this was his way of telling her that it was okay to miss Joe, and that he would never resent her for whatever feelings she had for her former husband. God, how she loved her mate, this man who she knew would always be there for her and their pup.

He stared down intently at the name etched into the smooth stone. "You loved her first, I can never take that away. And I wouldn't want to. Because if it wasn't for you, she wouldn't have learned to believe in love in the first place. So, thank you for that."

They stood in the silence for a long time, among the lush green surroundings and only the faint chirping of birds or the scuttle of squirrels breaking the tranquility. There was no need for more words, as Delacroix had spoken for them and said everything that was necessary.

"I'm glad we came here," she said, wiping her tears with the back of her hand.

"Thank you." He pressed a kiss to her forehead and nuzzled her cheek, then splayed a hand over her bump.

"We should head out," she said. "We have some very important people waiting for us."

———

Instead of going back to Manhattan, they drove to LaGuardia Airport, which was only a few miles from the cemetery. After leaving the car in the parking garage, they waited in the main arrivals area in the terminal building, scanning the doors that separated them from the concourses where the passengers were deplaning.

Delacroix crossed his arms over his chest and tapped his fingers on his bicep. The flight was only thirty minutes delayed, but he couldn't help but feel impatient.

"Don't worry," Mika said. "They'll be here soon."

As if her words conjured them up, the automatic doors whooshed open, and Gabrielle, Marina, and Adelaide stepped out.

"*Mémère!*" he called as they strode over to the trio. He bent down and kissed his grandmother's cheeks as Mika embraced Gabrielle and Marina. "How was the flight?" He'd been nervous because it was Adelaide's first time flying, as she'd never left Louisiana in her entire life.

"It was interestin'," she said with a smile. "I never thought I'd ever get to ride in a plane."

He hugged his aunt and cousin. "And did you enjoy it?" he asked the teen.

"Everyone was nice," Marina said, her eyes wide and hands clapping together. "But I can't believe we're in New York. I've only seen it in pictures."

"We'll have plenty of time for sightseein'." Gabrielle's eyes turned serious. "We should get to our meeting. I'm sure we'll have plenty to talk about."

They led the Beaumonts to the car, and soon, they were on their way.

Marina let out squeaks of excitement as they crossed over the Manhattan Bridge and saw the New York skyline. "The buildings ... everything ... they're all so big."

Delacroix smiled to himself, remembering the first time

he had seen it all. Of course, the circumstances were much different, as Nick Vrost had picked him up from a rest stop in the middle of nowhere in New Jersey. But there was the same sense of excitement as soon as he saw the skyline—it was that feeling that things were about to change, and now, looking at Mika, he couldn't help but feel wonder at how much things *had* changed, and all for the better. Though his past molded him, now there was only the future to look forward to.

They arrived at Fenrir Corp. headquarters and headed up to the executive level floors. Adelaide, Gabrielle, and Marina were not only invited to New York to visit him and Mika, but because they were about to do something very important. As soon as his grandmother had learned about the mages, she was eager to join the fight. "We can't just do nothin'. They haven't come after us, but they soon will, and I'll be damned if we don't strike first," she had said.

Almost everyone was there when they entered the Alpha's office—Lucas Anderson, of course, as well as his sister, Adrianna Anderson. Daric stood in a corner, chatting quietly with the dragon himself, Sebastian Creed. Mika's parents were sitting on the couch, while Jacob, Arch's father Killian, and Lizzie were sitting opposite them. Arch and Cliff stood off to the side.

The only one missing from GI was Wyatt, but then again, where Lizzie was, he usually, well, *wasn't*. It seemed strange to him because after Mika was hurt, he never wanted to leave her side ever again, but Wyatt's reaction was the opposite. Since the incident at the carnival, he avoided Lizzie, stopped stalking her office or even following her with his gaze if they were in the same room together. Maybe his suspicions about the two of them were wrong, but he'd been so sure, especially after hearing that Jean-Baptiste had sustained mysterious bruises and cuts while he had been in their custody. He glanced at his grandmother, and wondered if it would be ethical to ask her if she could tell if Lizzie and Wyatt were True Mates so he could start a betting pool.

Lucas stood up and walked over to greet them. "Welcome to New York, Ms. Beaumont," he said. "My name is Lucas Anderson, Alpha of New York. Thank you for coming all the way here to see us."

Adelaide peered up at him, then looked around. "Hmmm ... I can see the appeal. Seems they grow all Lycans big and handsome," she cackled. "If I was thirty years younger—"

"Mama," Gabrielle admonished. "Sorry, she's not usually like this. I'm Gabrielle Beaumont, and this is my daughter, Marina."

Lucas took their offered hands and glanced at the teen. "Perhaps you'd like a tour of the shopping center downstairs while we have our meeting, Marina? I can have one of the staff—"

"Just because she's only thirteen doesn't mean she can't help." Adelaide's face grew serious. "Besides, I'm growing old, and my power is fading ... that's the price of dark magic, I'm afraid. But Marina, soon she will be all you have left. She will need to learn now before I am gone."

Delacroix reached out to his grandmother. "Surely it'll be a while—"

"*Bah*, don't coddle me, child. I'm nearly ninety." But she smiled up at him. "Don't worry, I'll still be here to see your *bebes*. Nothing will stop me from holding my great-grandchild." She turned back to Lucas. "Marina's much more sensitive than I, and her power is only growing. She can help you track what you've been looking for. Go ahead, *ma chevrette.*" She patted Marina's shoulder. "Show them."

Marina looked around the room. "So much ... glowing." She pointed to Lucas and Adrianna. "Your mates aren't here, but I can see your glow. Same there," she gestured to the couch where Killian sat with Jacob and Lizzie.

Before Delacroix could ask which one of the three she meant, Marina continued. "Oh, no." Her nose wrinkled at Arch and Cliff. She shook her head. "No one yet." Then she walked to Alynna and Alex, waving her hand between them, like she was touching something. "Oh, yes. Yes. The thread. So beautiful." Then she headed toward Daric and Sebastian, and she let out a gasp. "You both have the glow but ... you're not Lycans." She bit her lip. "You're something ... big," she said to Sebastian. "And you ..."

"What am I, little one?" Daric asked, his eyes amused.

"You're like us, but different." Her eyes scrunched up at him, and she took his hands. "Oh. You touched something. Something ..." Her breath came in small pants. "I don't know ... it's like your hands ... they have stains ..." Her face went pale. "So much death ... I ..."

"Shhh ..." Gabrielle pulled her back. "It's okay, it's okay."

"Mama ... it's so terrible," she sobbed into her mother's arms. "So much blood."

Daric's eyes turned stormy. "Before coming here, I transported the dagger," he said, referring to the one artifact of Magus Aurelius that the Lycans possessed. The mages had another—a necklace, while a third was lost, which is what Daric and his son Cross had been looking for. "We change its hiding place every now and then."

"You can really see it?" Lucas asked Marina.

"We both can," Adelaide said. "The dark sight shows us the presence of magic, and in the case of powerful objects, traces of it." Her small body shook as if a chill passed over her. "That object ... whatever it was ... bad *gris-gris*. Blood magic."

"The artifacts of Magus Aurelius were infused with the blood of three hundred Lycans and three hundred humans," Daric said. "The mages plan to use all three to bring darkness and destruction to the world."

"Ah." The old woman's head bobbed up and down. "Three is a special number when it comes to magic, *oui*? Three artifacts. Three hundred humans. Three hundred Lycans." She thought for a moment. "Just as I feared. Now, we must work together to find it. Whatever the Beaumonts can do to help, we will do it."

"Thank you," Lucas said, bowing his head. "We appreciate any help you can give us." He motioned for them to take their seats on the third empty couch in the room. "Now, I have some good news, at least. We've made some progress in tracking down how the mages are able to fund their activities. Lizzie?"

The redhead stood up and took a tablet computer from her bag, facing it to the room. "It took a lot of work—I mean *a lot* of work, exhausting every favor I had and owing a couple more people, but I was able to trace the funds the mages have been using. The money's been funneled into layers and layers of shell companies in the Bahamas, Lichtenstein, Estonia, Cyprus, and Cayman Islands." She shoved her tablet forward and names began to scroll along the screen. "I was able to trace the sources from a couple of companies, most of which are owned by these people."

Arch craned his neck forward, eyes squinting. "Peter Kyrakolous ... Irina Alekperova ... Sir James Dalton ... J.S. Strohen ... Bertrand Pinault ... that's like a list of Forbes's Richest People."

"I know, right?" Lizzie said. "But the paper trail doesn't lie. Somehow, the mages were able to convince these people to 'donate' to their cause."

"It's not farfetched," Lucas said. "They do have the necklace. That means—"

"Apologies for the delay."

All eyes turned to the door, not because it opened, but because someone had materialized in front of it. It was Cross Jonasson, Daric's hybrid son. He looked just like his father—tall, Viking-like, with long blond hair though the sides of his head were shaved, and he sported a scraggly thick beard. Like his father, he possessed powers that allowed him to move across long distances and materialize almost anywhere. Delacroix had previously met him in Zhobghadi when they rescued King Karim from his enemies and the mages.

"I had some business to attend to." Cross strode forward. "Primul," he said, acknowledging Lucas. "I have—"

Marina shrieked. "You too!"

"What's wrong?" Gabrielle asked.

"He's ... he's ..." Her face scrunched up in determination as she walked toward Cross. The hybrid seemed frozen to the spot and didn't stop the young girl from coming closer or taking his hand. "You've touched something bad, too."

Daric frowned. "No, only I have touched the dagger."

"But his hands," Marina cried. "His hands." She stared up at him. "You've touched it too and ..." She frowned. "What's wrong with your glow?"

"She's right," Adelaide said. "You've touched something very powerful. It's similar to what stains the warlock's hand, but different."

"Cross?" Lucas's voice was tight. "What is she saying?"

"Son." Daric came forward, his face inscrutable. "What's the meaning of this?"

The atmosphere in the room became thick as molasses. Delacroix held on to Mika's hand and she squeezed back. His wolf was going crazy, hackles raised and ready for action. He didn't know what was going on, but if there was something wrong, he had to get her out of here.

Cross's expression remained neutral. "I don't know what you're talking about."

"She," Lucas nodded at Marina, "can detect traces of magic. And she knows you've touched it."

"Touched what?" Cross asked nonchalantly.

"The *artifact*, son." Daric raised his voice, a rare occurrence for the normally calm warlock. "You've touched the ring of Magus Aurelius, haven't you?"

"You have it?" The air crackled with the power of Lucas's wolf. "All this time, you've had it?" His eyes glowed as his wolf reached for the surface.

Cross's nostrils flared as he seemed to struggle to keep his stoic mask in place. "It's not ... it's not what you think."

"What the hell are we supposed to think?" Lucas took a step toward him. "You've been keeping it from us and—"

"I'm sorry," he said, turning his head to his father. "But you have to understand ..."

Lucas let out a growl and lunged at Cross, but he only got air. The hybrid had disappeared into thin air. "Goddamn ...

get him," he said to Daric, his voice deadly. "I don't care if he's your son, I want him back here."

Daric seemed to hesitate, but nodded. "Yes, Primul." And then he shimmered away.

"I don't understand, *Mémère*." Marina's blonde brows were drawn into a frown. "Did you see it? Why did his glow look like that?"

"I don't know." Adelaide clucked her tongue. "But I did not like the look of it."

Adrianna Anderson came up to Lucas and put a hand on his shoulder, trying to calm him down. "Lucas ... I can't believe it. How? Did he have it all this time?"

Lucas seemed to struggle to keep his wolf in control. "I don't know, but we'll find out."

Delacroix felt his mate tug at his hand. "There's something else going on," Mika whispered to him. "I can't ... I don't believe Cross would do something like this without good reason."

"People aren't always what they seem, *cher*," he said.

"Yes, but Cross ..." She shook her head. "I've known him for so long. And fought beside him. There has to be some explanation."

Around them, all the Lycans' emotions varied, ranging from worried to agitated to confused. Did Cross really have the ring all this time? Had he just been pretending to search for it? And of course, the biggest question was *why*?

"We will find out," he said to his mate. He placed a hand on her stomach, on the life she nurtured inside her. At the beginning of all this, he had thought he had no skin in this game, that there was nothing at stake for him. But now, things had indeed changed. He had to fight; fight for her, fight for their child, so that it could have a future. And God help anyone who tried to harm them.

Mika placed her hand over his and looked up at him with those emerald eyes. "Together," she said.

"Yes." He couldn't shield her or change what she was. Mika would always be out there, fighting for what was right. It was what he admired and loved most about her. But he would always be by her side, for now and always.

———

Thank you for reading! I hope you enjoyed this chapter of the True Mates Generations series

I have some extra HOT bonus scenes for you that weren't featured in this book - just join my newsletter here to get access:

http://aliciamontgomeryauthor.com/mailing-list/

You'll get access to ALL the bonus materials from all my books and my **FREE** novella **The Last Blackstone Dragon.**

ABOUT THE AUTHOR

Alicia Montgomery has always dreamed of becoming a romance novel writer. She started writing down her stories in now long-forgotten diaries and notebooks, never thinking that her dream would come true. After taking the well-worn path to a stable career, she is now plunging into the world of self-publishing.

 facebook.com/aliciamontgomeryauthor
twitter.com/amontromance
bookbub.com/authors/alicia-montgomery

Made in the USA
Las Vegas, NV
27 November 2023

81685496R00163